Jan Morris, who is Anglo-Welsh by parentage, divides her time between her library-house in North Wales, her *dacha* in the Black Mountains of South Wales, and travel abroad. She has been to Manhattan every year since 1953, makes an annual visit to Venice, and has spent much of her life wandering and writing for (mostly American) magazines.

Her books include the *Pax Britannica* trilogy (*Heaven's Command*, *Pax Britannica*, and *Farewell the Trumpets*), the autobiographical *Conundrum* and *Pleasures of a Tangled Life*, and seven volumes of travel essays, *Venice*, *Oxford*, *Spain*, *The Matter of Wales*, *Among the Cities*, *Manhattan '45* and *Hong Kong: Xianggang*. She has also edited *The Oxford Book of Oxford* and two Welsh anthologies. Her first work of fiction, *Last Letters from Hav* was shortlisted for the Booker Prize. Many of her books are published by Penguin.

LAST LETTERS FROM HAV

JAN MORRIS

PENGUIN BOOKS

PENGUIN BOOKS

Published by the Penguin Group
Penguin Books Ltd, 27 Wrights Lane, London W8 5TZ, England
Penguin Books USA Inc., 375 Hudson Street, New York, New York 10014, USA
Penguin Books Australia Ltd, Ringwood, Victoria, Australia
Penguin Books Canada Ltd, 2801 John Street, Markham, Ontario, Canada L3R 1B4
Penguin Books (NZ) Ltd, 182–190 Wairau Road, Auckland 10, New Zealand

Penguin Books Ltd, Registered Offices: Harmondsworth, Middlesex, England

First published by Viking 1985
Published in Penguin Books 1986
10 9 8 7 6 5 4 3 2

Copyright © Jan Morris, 1985
All rights reserved

Printed in England by Clays Ltd, St Ives plc
Typeset in Plantin

CONTENTS

But what if light and shade should be reversed?
If you press the switch then, will you turn the darkness on?

Avzar Melchik, *Bağlılık* ('Dependence')

The names of living persons in this book have mostly been fictionalized, but inevitably some characters will be recognized anyway. I apologize, and hope they will not feel I have betrayed their trust or abused their hospitality.

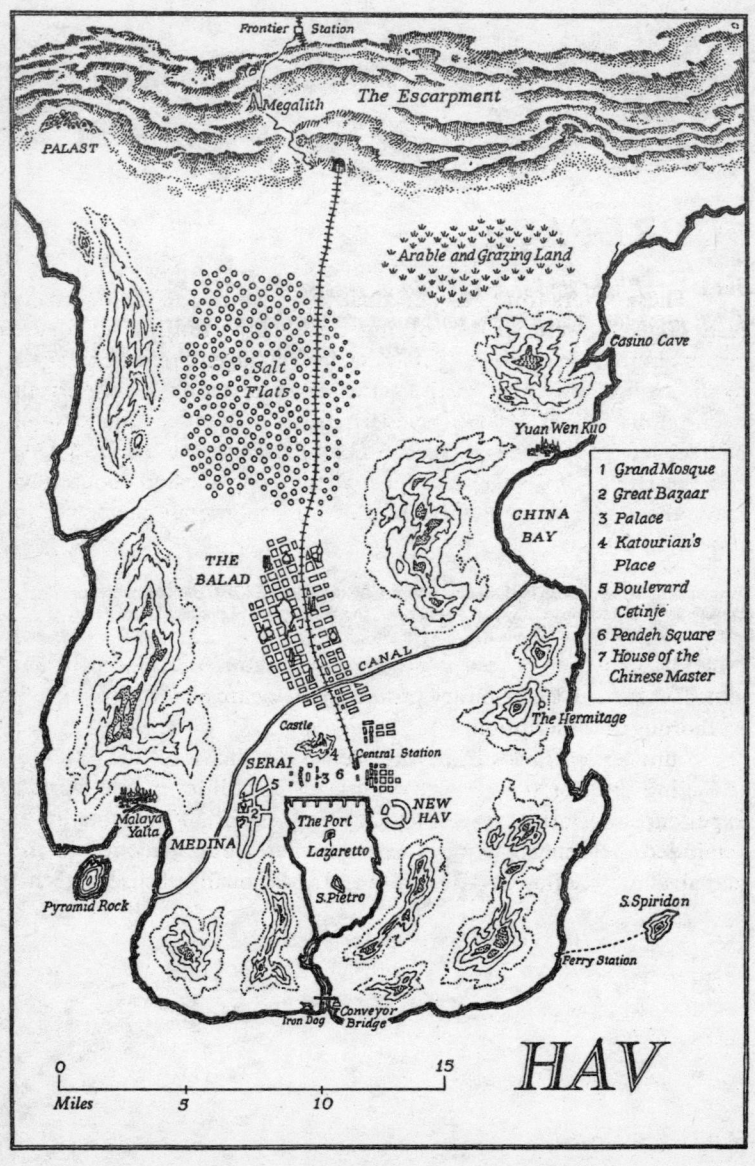

Frontier ○ Station

The Escarpment

Megalith

PALAST

Arable and Grazing Land

Casino Cave

Salt Flats

Yuan Wen Kuo

THE BALAD

CHINA BAY

1 Grand Mosque
2 Great Bazaar
3 Palace
4 Katourian's Place
5 Boulevard Cetinje
6 Pendeh Square
7 House of the Chinese Master

CANAL

The Hermitage

Castle

Central Station

SERAI

5 □ 4 3 6

NEW HAV

Malaya Yalta

MEDINA

The Port Lazaretto

Pyramid Rock

S. Pietro

S. Spiridon

Ferry Station

Iron Dog Conveyor Bridge

0   15

Miles   5   10

HAV

PREFACE

These letters from Hav, originally contributed to the magazine *New Gotham*, were written during the months leading up to the events, in the late summer of 1985, which put an end to the character of the city. They thus constitute the only substantial civic portrait ever published, at least in modern times. Countless visitors, of course, left passing descriptions. They marvelled at the Iron Dog and the House of the Chinese Master, they pontificated about New Hav, they caught something of the atmosphere in memoirs, in novels, in poetry –

> . . . *the green-grey shape that seamen swear is Hav,*
> *Beyond the racing tumble of its foam.*

Nobody, however, wrote a proper book about the place. It was almost as though a conspiracy protected the peninsula from too frank or thorough a description.

I count myself lucky in having seen it for the first time late in a travelling life, for it was itself a little compendium of the world's experience, historically, aesthetically, even perhaps spiritually. It reminded me constantly of places elsewhere, but remained to the end absolutely, often paradoxically and occasionally absurdly itself.

MARCH

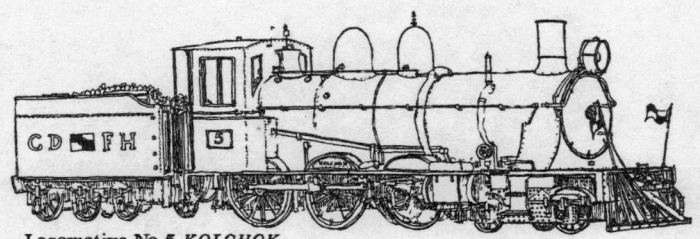

Locomotive No.5 *KOLCHOK*

1

At the frontier – the tunnel pilot – L'Auberge Impériale – morning calls

I did what Tolstoy did, and jumped out of the train when it stopped in the evening at the old frontier. Far up at the front the engine desultorily gasped, and wan faces watched me through crusted carriage windows as I walked all alone down the platform to the gate. There was no pony trap awaiting me of course (Tolstoy's reminded him sadly of picnics at Yasnaya Polyana), but a smart enough green Fiat stood in the station yard, a young man in sun-glasses and a blue blazer beckoned me from the wheel, and in no time we were off along the rutted track towards the ridge.

Very unusual, said the driver, to find a customer at the station these days, but he made the journey twice a week anyway, there and back, under contract to the railway. This was the tunnel pilot's car, he explained, and he was Yasar Yeğen the tunnel pilot's nephew, the pilotage being a hereditary affair. In his great-grandfather's time they had done the trip with a pony cart, and in those days, when the tunnel was considered one of the wonders of the world, all manner of great swells used to leave the train up there for the experience of the spectacle. Why did they need a pilot for the tunnel? The Porte had insisted on it, for southbound trains only, as a token of the Sultan's sovereignty after the Pendeh settlement; and ever since then, for more than a century, while Porte, Sultan and Czars too had all passed into history, a member of the Yeğen family had boarded the Mediterranean Express at the frontier stop, and formally ushered it through the escarpment.

Dust billowed behind us as we bounced over the snow-streaked plateau; ahead of us there stood a solitary tall stone, a megalith upon a mound; and then suddenly we were on the rim of the great declivity, and over it, and plunging down the ancient and spectacular mule-track, the celebrated 'Staircase', which appears in all the old engravings crowded with pack-trains, wandering dervishes, beggars squatting on rocks, platoons of soldiers with pikes and muskets, great ladies veiled in palanquins, vastly turbanned dragomans and gentlemanly horsemen in fly-netted pith helmets – 'a very inconvenient approximation', as Kinglake called it, 'of Jacob's Ladder'. The coming of the railway ended all that, and now the track was altogether empty – hardly anybody used it, Yasar Yeğen told me, except Adventure Tours in four-wheel-drive buses, and the cave-dwellers who inhabited the western face of the escarpment. So we proceeded gloriously unimpeded, skidding helter-skelter around those once-famous zigzags, and occasionally evading them with boisterous short cuts between the outcrops.

Halfway down I looked back, and there I saw, issuing from a squat chimney near the crown of the cliff, a pillar of black smoke which showed that the Express was on its way, chuffing subterraneously down its own spiralling descent within the limestone. 'Don't worry,' said Yasar, 'I am never late,' and sure enough, when we slithered to a showy stop on the gravelly clearing at the tunnel mouth, it was only a few minutes before we heard the train's resonant wailing cry from the bowels of the mountain. A gust of sooty smoke out of the big black hole – a cyclopean eye groping through the murk – a powerful emanation of steam, grease and coal dust – and there it was, tremendously emerging from its labyrinth, a huge locomotive of dirty red with a cowcatcher and a brass bell, its crew leaning from each side of their cab, as they reached the daylight, wearing goggles and greasy cloth caps, but bearing themselves as grandly as ships' officers on their flying bridges. The train eased itself to a stop with a mighty hissing of brakes, steam and smoke, and beneath the numerals on its cab I could just make out, not quite obliterated even now, the old Cyrillic characters of the Imperial Russian Railways.

A tall elderly man swung himself from the footplate, wearing a sober dark suit, remarkably unblemished, and a black felt hat in the Ataturk mode. He turned to salute the engine-driver when he reached the ground, and then walked in a distinctly authoritative way towards the Fiat. Hastily Yasar, smoothing his hair and blazer, jumped out of the car to open the back door, and almost involuntarily I got out too, so imposing was that approaching figure. The tunnel pilot looked as though the world and all its movement depended on him. The train seethed and simmered respectfully behind his back. He had a bristly grey moustache, possibly waxed, and on his chest he wore a brass emblem, larger than a mere medal, more like the insignia of some chivalric order, which incorporated, I saw as he neared me, the silhouetted form of a very old-fashioned steam engine. He strode directly over to me, bowed low and kissed my hand, grunting 'Dear lady' in a blurred and throaty sort of way, 'Dirleddy', as though he had often heard it said but had never analysed it. Then he stepped into his car, the door was closed gently behind him, and I hardly had time to thrust my money into Yasar's hand before they were away, hurling dust and rubble in their wake, breakneck up the precipitous bends of the escarpment. I sprinted for the train, dispassionately observed by those same pale faces in the carriage windows, and was just in time to scramble aboard before, with a more perfunctory hoot and a clang of couplings, it moved heavily off into the flatlands.

It was dusk by now as we crawled very, very slowly towards the city. Everything looked monotonous out there, and cold, and shadowy, and silent, and grey. We were crossing the marshy salt-flats which have always acted as a cordon sanitaire, and a field of fire too, between the coast settlements and the escarpment. They looked horribly forbidding, brackish wastelands bounded to the east by low brown hills – which one of them, I wondered, had Schliemann first claimed to be Troy? There was a line of tall iron windmills, and a few lights flickered palely in the marshes; and when, clattering over a bridge, we entered the first purlieus of the city, they too seemed sufficiently unwelcoming, with their shambolic buildings of mud-brick and clapboard, some painted a gloomy blue, with scrabbly yards, and clumps of corrugated iron shanties, and gravel football pitches here and there, and an occasional tall chimney, and dim unlit streets. Sometimes an open fire blazed, and a few figures crouched around it. More often everything in sight looked lifeless, perhaps abandoned.

The train moved so laboriously through these unlovely suburbs, frequently stopping altogether and ringing its bell mournfully all the way, that by the time we were in the city proper it was pitch dark. The lights outside were all very faint, and I could see nothing much but burly dark shapes in silhouette, a power station, a dome, a square tower, what looked like a minaret, and a general monumental mass: and so, well after midnight, we lurched at last exhaustedly, as though the rolling stock were all but worn out too, into the vestigially brighter lights of the Central Station, which seemed to be immense, but turned out to have, in the event, only the one platform. '*Hav!*' a great voice boomed. '*Hav Centrum!*'

In a matter of moments, it seemed to me, my few fellow-passengers had all scuttled away into the dark, and I was left alone upon the platform, wondering where to spend the rest of the night. But enormously facing me I saw an advertisement made, as in mosaic, of brightly coloured china tiles. On the right it offered a stylized depiction of Russia, onion domes, troikas, fir forests. On the left, bathed in golden sunshine against a cobalt sea, was the city of Hav, with elaborately hatted ladies and marvellously patrician beaux sauntering, a little disjointedly where the tiles met, along a palm-shaded corniche. Florid in the middle, in Russian Cyrillic, in Turkish Arabic and in French, a sign announced the presence of L'Auberge Impériale du Chemin de Fer Hav, and immediately below it a cavernous entrance invited me, along red-carpeted corridors lined with empty showcases, to a kiosk of glass and gilded iron-work in which there sat a stout woman, smiling, in black.

'You encountered the tunnel pilot, I hear,' she remarked unexpectedly when I presented my passport for registration. 'He is my cousin Rudolph. He was named, you may be interested to know, after a Crown Prince of Austria who came here long ago, and took the pony cart with my great-grandfather to see the train come from the tunnel.'

'Your family meets everyone.'

'*Used* to meet everyone, should we say? Whom did we not meet? All the crowned heads, all the great people, Bismarck, Nijinsky, Count Kolchok of course many, many times. You should see the pictures in the pilot's office at the frontier – everyone is there! Even Hitler came once, they say, though we did not know it at the time.

Our last great lady was Princess Grace – I met her myself, such a lovely person – they had a special car waiting for her, over from Izmir, they said it was the biggest car that ever went down the Staircase, even bigger than the Kaiser's . . .'

Chatting in this good-natured way, Miss Fatima Yeğen signed me in and showed me to my room, which was very large, like a salon, and had thick curtains of faded crimson. So, I thought as she stumped away down the corridor, late in a life of travel I am in Hav at last! A big blue and white samovar stood in the corner of the room, and there was a picture of a rural winter scene signed T. Ramotsky, 1879 – the very year, I guessed, when they had fitted out the Imperial Railway Hotel for its original guests. A palpable smell of eggs haunted the apartment, mingled with a suggestion of pomade, and when I drew the curtains there was nothing to be seen outside but the well of the hotel, lugubriously illuminated and echoing with the clatter of washing-up from a kitchen far below. At the foot of my bed was a television set, but when I turned it on it was showing a black-and-white Cary Grant film dubbed into Turkish; so I went to sleep instead – confusedly, as in a state of weightlessness, having no idea really what lay outside the walls of L'Auberge Impériale du Chemin de Fer Hav, and fancying only, in my half-waking dreams, the bubble of the samovar, the drab grey salt-flats, the windmills, and the procession of kings, dukes and chancellors winding their way with plumes of swirling soil, like defiances, down the mule-track from the frontier.

But I was awoken in the morning by two marvellous sounds as the first light showed through my shutters: the frail quavering line of a call to prayer, from some far minaret across the city, and the note of a trumpet close at hand, greeting the day not with a bold reveille, but more in wistful threnody.

2

Hardly had the last note of the trumpet died away than I was dressed and on my way down the silent hotel corridors towards the daylight.

The legend of the trumpet is this. When at the end of the eleventh century the knights of the First Crusade seized Hav from the Seljuks, they were joined by hundreds of Armenians flocking down from their beleaguered homelands in the north-west. Among them was the musician Katourian, and he became the cherished minstrel of the Court, celebrating its feats and tragedies in beloved ballads, growing old and grey in its service.

In 1191 Saladin, after a siege of three months, forced the surrender of the Crusaders, and on the morning of the Feast of St Benedict the Christians left the castle with full courtesies of war and marched to the galleys waiting in the harbour. Their Armenian followers were left to face the fury of the Muslims, and as the last of the long line of Franks passed through the castle gate between the rows of Arab soldiery, the musician Katourian, feeble and bent by now, appeared on the breastwork high above and sang, with more power and emotion even than in the heyday of his art, the most famous of all his great laments, 'Chant de doleure pour li proz chevalers qui sunt morz'. It rang across the city as a magnificent farewell, so the fable says, and with its last declining cadence Katourian plunged a dagger into his breast and died upon the rampart, known from that day to this as Katourian's Place.

Moved by the tragic splendour of this gesture, Saladin ordered that in honour of the minstrel, and of the Christian knights themselves, the lament should be sung each morning, from the same place, immediately after the call to prayer. The Arabs never did master the words of the song, which concerned the immolation of a group of otherwise forgotten Gascon men-at-arms, but the melody they subtly adapted until it sounded almost Muslim itself, and at dawn each day, throughout the long centuries of Islamic rule, it was sung from Katourian's Place. The British, during their half-century in Hav after the Napoleonic wars, substituted a trumpeter for the muezzin's voice; the Russians who followed honoured the old tradition, and the governors of the Tripartite Mandate, after them. And so it was that on my first morning I was hastening towards my opening revelation of the city to the echo of a dirge from the European Middle Ages.

I passed through the deserted station (the train still standing there lifeless) and stepped into the yellowish mist of the great square outside. I could hardly see across it – just a suggestion of great buildings opposite, and to my right the mass of the castle looming in a dim succession of stairs, terraces, curtain walls and gateways, only the very top of the immense central keep, Beynac's Keep, being touched with the golden sunshine of the morning. Though I could hear not far away a deep muffled rumble, as of an army moving secretly through the dawn, the square itself was utterly empty; but even as I stood there, striding down the last steps from the castle came the trumpeter himself, down from the heights, his instrument under his arm, huddled in a long brown greatcoat against the misty damp.

'*Merhaba* trumpeter!' I accosted him. 'I am Jan Morris from Wales, on my very first morning in Hav!'

He answered in kind. 'And I am Missakian the trumpeter,' he laughed. '*Merhaba*, good morning to you!'

'Missakian! You're Armenian?'

'But naturally. The trumpeters of Hav always are. You know the legend of Katourian? Well, then you will understand' – and after an exchange of pleasantries, expressing the hope that we might meet again, 'not quite so early in the morning, perhaps,' trumpet under his arm, he resumed his progress across the square.

*

Which reminded me, as the mist began to lift, of somewhere like Cracow or Kiev, so grey and cobbled did it seem to be, and so immense. It was hardly worth exploring then, so instead I followed that rumble, which seemed to have its focus somewhere away to my left, and found myself in a mesh of side-streets I knew not where, joining the extraordinary procession of traffic that makes its way each morning to Hav's ancient market on the waterfront. Pendeh Square, the great central plaza of the city, is closed to all traffic until seven in the morning, but the thoroughfares around it, I discovered, were already clogged with all manner of vehicles. There were pick-up trucks with brightly painted sides. There were motorbikes toppling with the weight of their loaded sidecars. There were private cars with milk-churns on their roofs. Men in wide straw hats and striped cotton *gallabiyehs* and women in headscarves and long black skirts lolloped along on pony carts, and a string of mules passed by, weighed down with firewood. They moved, for all the noise of their engines and the rattle of their wheels on the cobblestones, in a kind of hush, very deliberately; and I found myself caught up in the steady press of it, stared at curiously but without comment, until we all debouched into the wide market-place at the water's edge, where fishing-boats were moored bow to stern along the quay, and where as the sun broke through the morning fog all was already bustle and flow.

In every city the morning market, the very first thing to happen every day, offers a register of the public character. Few offer so violent a first impression as the waterside market of Hav. Apparently unregulated, evidently immemorial, it seemed to me that morning partly like a Marseilles fish-wharf, and partly like the old Covent Garden, and partly like a flea-market, for there seemed to be almost nothing, at six in the morning, that was not there on sale. Everything was inextricably confused. One stall might be hung all over with umbrellas and plastic galoshes, the next piled high with celery and boxes of edible grass. There were mounds of apples, artistically arranged, there were stacks of boots and racks of sunglasses and rows of old radios. There were spare parts for cars, suitcases with images of the Pyramids embossed upon them, rolls of silk, nylon underwear in yellows and sickly pinks, brass trays, Chinese medicines, hubble-bubbles, coffee beans in vast tin containers, souvenirs of Mecca or Istanbul, second-hand book stalls with grubby old volumes in many languages – I looked inside a copy of *Moby Dick*, and stamped within its covers were the words 'Property of the American University, Beirut'.

In a red-roofed shed near the water, shirtsleeved butchers were at work, chopping bloody limbs and carcasses, skinning sheep and goats before my eyes; and there were living sheep too, of a brownish tight-curled wool, and chickens in crude wicker baskets, and pigeons in coops. Women shawled and bundled against the cold sold cups of steaming soup. On the quay Greek fishermen offered direct from their boats fish still flapping in their boxes, mucous eels, writhing lobsters, prawns, urchins, sponges and buckets of what looked like phosphorescent plankton.

Almost any language, I discovered, would get you by in Hav – not just Turkish, but Italian, French, Arabic, English at a pinch, even Chinese. This was Pero Tafur's 'Lesser Babel'! Some people were dressed Turkish-style in sombre dark suits with cloth caps, many wore those wide hats and cotton robes, rather like North Africans, some were dark and gypsy-looking, a few were Indian, some were high-cheeked like Mongols, and some, long-haired and medieval of face, wearing drab mixtures of jeans, raincoats and old bits of khaki uniform, I took to be the Kretevs, the cave-dwellers of the escarpment. Tousled small dogs ran about the place; the Greeks on their boats laughed and shouted badinage to each other. Moving importantly among the stalls, treated with serious respect by the most bawdy of the fishermen, the most brutal of the butchers, I saw a solitary European, in a grey suit and a panama hat, who seemed to go about his business, choosing mutton here, fruit there, in a style that was almost scholarly.

He was followed by a pair of Chinese, who saw to it when their boss had made his decisions that his choice was picked from its tank, cut from its hook or removed unbruised from its counter, and placed in the porter's trolley behind; and I followed the little cortège through the meat market, along the line of the fishing-boats, to the jetty beyond the market. A spanking new motor-launch was moored there, blue and cream, like an admiral's barge, with a smart Chinese sailor in a blue jersey waiting at the wheel, and another at the prow with his boat-hook across his arms. Gently into the well, amidships, went the crates of victuals; the European adeptly stepped aboard; and with a snarl of engines the boat backed from the quay, turned in a wide foamy curve, and sped away down the harbour towards the sea.

'Good gracious,' I said to one of the Greeks, 'who was that?'

'That was Signor Biancheri, the chef of the Casino. Every morning he comes here. You've never heard of him? You surprise me.'

'You should go up to Katourian's Place,' the trumpeter had told me, 'but wait for an hour or two, until the sun comes up.' So now that the sun was rising above the silhouette of the castle, and its warm light was creeping along the quays and striking into the cobbled streets behind, I walked back across the still empty square and clambered up the steep stone steps to see for myself the city this remarkable populace had, over so many centuries, evolved for itself.

I passed through barbicans and curtain walls, I clambered up shattered casements, I entered the immense gateway upon which Saladin had caused to be carved his triumphant and celebrated proclamation: 'In the name of God, the Merciful, the Almighty, Salah ed Din the warrior, the defender of Islam, may God glorify his victories, here defeated, humiliated and spared the armies of the Infidel.' And immediately inside, on the half-ruined rampart beside the gate, I found a second inscription, in English, upon a stone slab. 'In memory,' it said, 'of Katourian the musician. Erected by subscription of the Officers of Her Majesty's Royal Regiment of Artillery in the Protectorate of Hav and the Escarpment, AD 1837. *Semper Fidelis*.'

On the platform beside the plaque, the very spot where Katourian is supposed to have killed himself, I spread out my map and looked down for the first time upon all Hav. The last morning vapours were dispersing, and the greyness of the night before was becoming, as the sun rode higher in the sky, almost unnaturally clear – the blue rim of the sea around, the low hillocks to west and east, the line of the escarpment, still in shadow, like a high wall in the distance. Salt gleamed white in the wide marshlands. There were patches of green crops and pasture to the north-east, and curving across the peninsula I could see the line of the canal cut by the Spartans during their long investment of Athenian Hav. Here and there around the coast, fishing-boats worked in twos and threes; rounding the southern point went the scud and spray of Signor Biancheri's provision launch, hastening home to breakfast.

Now I could get the hang of the place, for the castle stands on the bald hill which is the true centre of Hav, and which was for centuries the seat of its power too. To the north of it, away to the salt-flats, extended the hangdog suburb where Hav's multi-ethnic proletariat, Turkish, Arab, Greek, African, Armenian, lives in a long frayed grid of shacks and cabins. It was marked on my map as the Balad, and it looked altogether anonymous, blank like a labour camp but for the spike of a minaret here and there, one or two church towers and brick-work chimneys, a stagnant-looking lake in the middle of it and a power station spouting smoke at its southern end. The railway track cut a wide swathe through the Balad, and parallel to it ran a tram-line, about which in places swamped dense clusters of figures, some in brown or black, some in white robes – ah, and there came the first tram of the morning, pulling a trailer, already scrambled all over by a mass of passengers clinging to its sides and platforms. I watched its lurching progress south – through those shabby shanty-streets – past the power station – out of sight for a moment in the lee of the castle hill . . .

. . . and turning myself to follow it, I saw spread out before me downtown Hav around the wide inlet of its haven. To the west, at the other end of the castle ridge, stood the vestigial remains of the Athenian acropolis, its surviving columns shored up by ugly brick buttresses. Away to the south I fancied I could just make out the Iron Dog at the entrance to the harbour, and beside it the platform of the Conveyor Bridge was already swinging slowly across the water. A couple of ships lay at their moorings in the port; on the waterfront the market was still thronged and bustling. And at my feet lay the mass of the central city, the Palace, the brightly domed offices of government, the circular slab of New Hav, the narrow crannied streets and tall white blocks of the Medina.

A red light was flashing from the prison island in the harbour, but even as I watched, it was switched off for the day, and instantly a hooter somewhere sounded a long steady blast. Seven o'clock, Hav time! Immediately, as if gates had been unlocked or barriers removed, the first traffic of the day spilled into Pendeh Square below me, and soon the din of the market had spread across the whole city, and there reached me from all around the reassuring noises of urban life, the hoots and the revs, the shouts, the clanging bells, the blaring radio music. The fishing-boats of the market sailed away in raggety flotilla down the harbour. Sunshine flashed from the upperworks of the ships, and wherever I looked the streets were filling up, cars were on the move and shopkeepers were unlocking their doors for the day's business. A small figure appeared upon the roof of the Palace, beneath its gilded onion dome, and raised upon its flagstaff the black-and-white chequered flag of Hav (which looks bathetically like the winner's flag at a motor-race, but was chosen in 1924, I have been told, so as to be utterly unidentifiable with the flag of any one of the Mandatory Powers).

Down the hill I went. The cicadas were chortling in the grass now, and halfway down a woman with a satchel over her shoulder was scrabbling in the turf for herbs. The great square was full of life by the time I got down there – cars everywhere, a tram rattling past the station entrance, flower-sellers setting up their trays beside the equestrian statue of Czar Alexander II in the middle. Outside the Palace gates, between the palm trees, two sentries in red jackets and crinkly astrakhan hats stood guard with fixed bayonets on antique rifles. The flag flew ridiculously up above. When I reached the station entrance, and made my way towards the hotel, I looked through the glass door of the Café de la Gare, to my right, and there with his instrument upright on the table the trumpeter Missakian, head down, was deep into a pile of beans.

3

Settling in – the routine – at the Athenaeum – in a vaccum – who cares?

Here as anywhere one must settle in. One must adjust one's first impressions, which may indeed be perfectly accurate, but are sure to be partial. Already, I must say, that castle does not look quite so towering on its hill. Missakian's morning trumpet is not quite so heart-rendingly flawless as it sounded that first morning, and the TV, if still fond of old Hollywood in Turkish, turns out to transmit programmes too in French, Italian and Chinese, not to mention brand-new American soap operas in Arabic.

Seen and heard at least from residence in the railway hotel, Hav is a city of very settled habit, living to programmes that seem inflexible. Usages of routine – 'two o'clock sharp', 'as always', 'according to custom' – are much favoured by Havians. Crack of dawn comes the call to prayer and the trumpet, and soon afterwards I hear the cry of the first hawker; he sells hot oatcakes in the yard behind the station, baking them in a portable oven, and always seems to have plenty of customers – many people, Miss Yeğen tells me, make a breakfast of them before they go to work. Seven o'clock, the siren sounds, and almost at once I hear the ding-ding-ding of the first tram, clattering into Pendeh Square. At eight the angelus rings from the French cathedral, and then the steel shutters of the shops clang up, one after the other through the streets. Eleven o'clock sharp on Tuesdays and Thursdays – well, *generally* sharp – and a long blast of the steam-whistle proclaims the departure of the Mediterranean Express for Kars (or as it used to be, and still can be with minor interruptions, for Tiflis, Rostov and Moscow . . .).

At eleven-thirty *really* sharp, every day of the week, one can hear the muffled report of a gun from the prison island, San Pietro. Hav time being half an hour before St Petersburg time, ever since the days of Russian rule, eleven-thirty rather than noon has been the official centre of the Hav day, the moment when all official departments close for the midday break. The shop shutters rattle down again, the trams pause in their schedules, and for most of the people of Hav a rather heavy lunch is followed by three or four hours of idle siesta, even in the winter months – until as the evening begins to draw in everything starts up all over again.

The prison gun goes off once more at half-past eight in the evening, and the working day is over. Nowadays, those who do not go home to supper with TV linger on till ten or eleven in the cafés and restaurants of New Hav, or go out to dinner in Yuan Wen Kuo, where things stay open later, or find disreputable indulgences, so Miss Yeğen says, in the back-streets of the Medina and Balad slums. But I am told that in the old days the climax or focal point of the evening, at least in the summer season, was the midnight arrival of the Express, to disgorge its complement of grandees and celebrities before a wondering crowd at the platform barricade. Now the train seldom arrives before two or three in the morning: and by then, as we know, nobody is awake in Hav but Miss Yeğen in her cubicle at the hotel.

One must also settle in, here as everywhere, in the official or administrative sense. This has proved a surprisingly pleasant experience. 'You must go to the Serai,' said Miss Yeğen, 'and register at the Aliens Registration Office, or else *zam*, you will be on my cousin's train without a first-class ticket, on your way to Kars.' So I went along to the Aliens Office, round the back of the government buildings, and there, presenting my passport and Evidence of Solvency (namely my American Express credit card, which so far as I know is accepted by nobody here), I met Mr Mahmoud Azzam, Deputy Controller of Aliens.

'Dirleddy,' said Mr Mahmoud Azzam – for this form of address, I now realize, is generic to courtly gentlemen of Hav, whatever their language – 'I see you are a writer. So am I, when I am not being Deputy Controller of Aliens, and you really must allow me, since it is now almost eleven-thirty, to introduce you to some of our confrères. Do please take lunch with me in what you might call our headquarters, the Athenaeum Club – just around the corner.' Mr Azzam was in his late twenties, I would judge, and rather progressive of appearance, having long sideburns and a droopy moustache, besides wearing in his lapel a badge saying in Turkish *Balinaları Öldürmeyin*, 'Save the Whale'. He did not look Athenaeum material, so to speak, especially when, having packed away his files and put his three or four pens in his breast pocket, he took me round the corner and I saw the club-house before me. It was built by the Russians, and looked all you would expect of an Athenaeum, dorically pillared on a single floor, grandly porticoed, green-shuttered, Minerva-crowned of course – in short, if a little down-at-heel, distinctly of the literary or scholarly élite. Was this really Mr Azzam, I wondered? No less pertinently, I mused, eyeing my own dusty sandals and less than immaculate slacks, was it entirely me?

But I need not have worried. Hardly had we climbed the front steps, entered the tall portico (bees' nests clustered under its eaves), and pushed open the big front door, when a comforting hubbub reached us – loud talk, much laughter, even snatches of singing. 'We are all intellectuals here,' said Mr Azzam, as though that explained everything, and thus encouraged, holding my copy of Braudel's *The Mediterranean in the Age of Philip II*, Volume II, as if in credential, I accompanied him into the maelstrom.

The whole of the ground floor of the Hav Athenaeum, which I surmise was once hall, dining-room, bar and silent library, is now a gigantic kind of common-room, as in some extremely avant-garde university. Cafeteria, bar, sitting-room, office, library, seemed to be strewn at random around this immense chamber. All was in a state of exuberant vigour. Everyone was talking very loudly, as at a cocktail party, except for those bent over books and magazines in the library wing, and there were knots of people arguing and gesticulating over drinks, and people shouting to one another from one end of the cafeteria queue to the other. Even the elderly women behind the counter replied to orders in screeching fortissimi. It was not at all how I imagined an Athenaeum.

And another un-Athenaeum-like thing: hardly anybody there, except the counter-women and me, seemed much more than thirty years old. Men and women, they looked like so many students – not even associate professors, I thought, at the most research graduates. They greeted me very breezily as we elbowed our way through. 'Hello old thing,' said a man in big horn-rimmed glasses, provoking a storm of 'Hush', 'Anton, so rude', and 'Take no notice, dirleddy', and from a young woman behind us in the queue came the cry 'Braudel! That monster!'

I asked her afterwards, when we came to share a table, why she cherished this exotic antipathy – it is not common, after all, to feel so fiercely about illustrious scholars.

'Why, because in God knows how many pages of God knows how many volumes, he never even recognizes the *existence* of Hav.'

This raised ardent waves of assent from our companions – 'shame, shame', 'quite true', 'notorious', etc. 'Fair play, Magda,' said Mahmoud Azzam, 'surely he mentions us in footnotes?'

She ignored him. 'And do you know why?' she asked me urgently, looking me very close and hard in the face. 'Because the French wish to refuse our being. They do not wish us to have existed. They failed to keep us after their infamous occupation in 1917, and so they want us not to be. They are a very jealous people. They know Hav has been for centuries, for aeons, a centre of art and civilization – long before France was thought of! – so if they cannot have us, and pretend us to be French, like Guadeloupans, or what-have-yous in the Pacific Sea, then they do not want us to be.'

A frenzied discussion followed this outburst, some supporting Magda, some telling me to take no notice of her, some declaring the Italians to be much worse than the French, some blaming the Americans, some fondly remembering visits to Paris, some going on to talk about wine, or Sartre, or Yves Saint Laurent ('You have met Yves? he is my hero') . . . 'We are intellectuals you see,' Mahmoud bawled in my ear. 'There is no subject that we cannot discuss, and all subjects make us angry.'

So now I am a member of the Athenaeum – it will make me feel at home, Mahmoud says. More than that, I am a colleague of Mahmoud and Magda and the man with the horn-rimmed glasses, whose name is Dr Borge, and so, despite my age, a temporary member of the intellectual establishment. Why *were* they all so young? I ventured to ask the other day, and there was a short silence before Mahmoud replied, 'Ah, well, you see in 1978 there were certain scandals here, and the leaders of the affair – the Prefects? is that the word in English? – they were all members of the Athenaeum. Many, many members, most of the older ones, resigned then.'

'Huh,' said Magda, 'or were *made* to resign . . .'

I asked no more. I knew my place. Still, I wonder what *did* happen in 1978? I wonder who the Prefects were?

Hav days pass swiftly, but somehow hazily. I know of nowhere in the world where the purpose of life seems so ill-defined. It is perfectly true that in the past Hav has played an exceedingly important role in history – has sometimes seemed indeed, as Magda would claim, the very centre of affairs, a crux, a junction of great traffic, not just the run-down terminal of the preposterously anachronistic Mediterranean Express. Especially down at the harbour, I can often imagine the days when the dhows and galleys lay alongside in a clamour of commerce, and the camel caravans from remotest Central Asia, all bales, and straw, and buckets, and ropes, and arguing Turcomans in long robes, assembled sprawled and grunting on the quays beside the warehouses!

But those purposes have long gone, and more than any other city I know Hav seems to live in a hazy vacuum. They used to say of Beirut that, just as aerodynamically a bumble-bee has no right to fly, so Beirut had no logical claim to survival. Even more is it true of contemporary Hav, which has no visible resources but the salt and the fish, which makes virtually nothing, which offers no flag of convenience, but yet manages to stagger on if not richly, at least without destitution.

History has left Hav behind, and our own times too, like Professor Braudel, have wilfully ignored the place. Its modern reputation is murky. Its political situation, vague enough even when you are in the city, is a blur indeed to the world at large. There is no airport, no proper highway into the peninsula, no harbour deep enough for big ships, and only a trickle of tourists ever bothers to make the long and extremely inconvenient journey on the train. Not one foreign news agency or newspaper maintains a correspondent in Hav. Only the British have a consul here, though the Turks possess their own Delegation Office in the Serai, and Hav has no missions abroad.

Were it not for the vessels in the harbour, the train twice a week, and the vapour trails of the airliners flying high overhead to Damascus, Teheran and the further East, it would often feel as though the place occupied its own entirely separate plane of existence, insulated against everywhere else.

All this makes the ponderous routine of Hav seem strangely introspective. Who cares, one soon comes to feel? Who cares if Missakian sounds his trumpet on the rampart? Who cares if the train is late, or what the Prefects did? Who cares if the gun goes off? Only the city itself, whose memories are so long, whose character is so elaborately creased or layered, and into whose idiosyncratic attitudes I find myself all too easily adapting.

4

*My apartment – the Serai – bureaucrats – legations– the King of
Montenegro – guards and a victim*

Less than a month in Hav, and I feel myself a citizen already.
I write now at my table upon the balcony of my own small apartment
– bedroom, dining-room with fringed velveteen table cover, kitchen,
bathroom whose magnificent shower, entitled 'Il Majestico', is tiled
with majolica flowers and fruits. Above me lives my landlady,
Signora Emilia Vattani, below me are the consulting rooms of an
elderly Lebanese psychiatrist, and below that again is the Ristorante
Milano, formerly I am told one of the best restaurants in the city,
now just a genial Egyptian coffee shop.

If I go up to the roof of the house, where Signora V maintains a
genteel garden, with a pergola and two urns, I can see protruding
above the rooftops to the west the spirally gilded onion domes of the
Serai, the very centre of all life in Hav. The Russians built it, of
course, as a deliberate expression of their own expansionism, but the
great complex long ago became an exclamation óf Hav's own proud
if ambivalent personality, and stands towards the city today as the
Eiffel Tower does to Paris, or the opera house to Sydney.

You know how curiously separate the Vatican feels, within the
enveloping tumult of Rome? Well, the Serai is rather like that. It also
reminds me of the Forbidden City in Beijing, old Peking, that
fantastic retreat of the Emperors which the Communists have turned
into the most extraordinary of public parks; for though in Russian
times the Serai was closed to all but grandees and officials, and the
public was kept at bay by formidable Cossacks, nowadays anybody

can walk through its gardens, which provide indeed an agreeable short cut from Pendeh Square to the Medina. Often I take a picnic lunch there, and eat my salami and oatcake on a bench immediately outside the Governor's Palace, in what was His Excellency's private pleasance. It is still dingily delightful, with fountains sporadically spouting, arbours, gravel walks, and in one corner a little *cottage orné*, now used as a potting shed, which was built by one of the early Russian governors as a present for his wife.

One hears tales of stately receptions here, with the wide french windows of the downstairs rooms open to the evening air, a military band playing on the terrace and half the nobility of Russia gossiping and flirting in those arbours. Tolstoy was a guest at such a function in 1885, and got into a furious argument with a cocksure captain of artillery, though in his second autobiography he simply says that he found the society of Hav 'unappealing'. Rimsky-Korsakov, on the other hand, who arrived here as an officer on a Russian warship two years later, was enchanted with everything he saw, played one of his own compositions on a grand piano in that very garden, and years later adapted the melody of the Hav trumpet call for the recurrent theme in *Scheherazade*.

No ravishing tunes sound through the garden now, but still the atmosphere of the place is genial. The governors of Hav are elected for five-year terms of office, generally towards the end of their careers as State Councillors, and to judge by photographs are usually portly gents of aldermanic style. I have not yet met the present incumbent, but once when Fatima Yeğen and I were sitting beside the fountains during her lunch break from the hotel we saw him emerge upon the balcony on the *piano nobile*, looking comfortably replete and holding a champagne glass in his hand. He caught sight of us and raised his glass. We waved. 'Such a charming man,' said Fatima. 'When he was younger he was the handsomest man in Hav, bar nobody.'

The Palace and its gardens are flanked, right and left, by the offices of the administration, each with four onion domes to balance the grand central dome of the residence. The whole ensemble looks like a cross between the Brighton Pavilion and St Basil's Cathedral in Red Square, and forms an anomalously exuberant centrepiece to the city. Though the candy colours of the domes are a little muted now, by dusty age and neglect, still seen down the streets of New Hav, or through the tumbled alleys of the Medina, when the sun is right they seem to shimmer there like huge billowing screens of silk. This fanciful and light-hearted ambiance is strikingly at odds with what goes on beneath them, for I doubt if there are any government offices more morosely addled with bureaucracy than the administrative offices of Hav.

Ostensibly they are divided into ministerial sections. Actually, since it was the enlightened idea of the Imperial Russian Government to house all its officials on huge open-plan floors, two to each block, everything seems to have spilled over long ago into everything else, and it is almost impossible to know, if you have business to transact there, in what department you are at any one moment. Come with me now, for instance, into the ground-floor offices of the North Block, nominally the precincts of the Hav Census, the Salt Administration, the Arable and Pasture Board, the Office of Languages and the Muslim Department of Wakfs. Entering this room is rather as I imagine entering the hospital at Scutari might have been, before Miss Nightingale got there. Even in the middle of the morning it is dark inside, and scattered bare electric light bulbs burn, giving everything a cavernous or cellar-like appearance. Hundreds of electric fans are massed in clusters on long rods from the ceiling, and the windows are covered with loose matting to keep the sun out. The entire room is filled with a mass of identical wooden desks, several hundred of them surely. Some are protected by makeshift partitions, of plyboard, cardboard or even loose canvas, while others are walled about with piles of books and ledgers. Many have been enmeshed in electric wires, plugged into light sockets above, which hang down like life-support systems to provide power for kettles, radios or winter heaters, while over them all runs a complicated pattern of pneumatic message tubes.

At every single desk a man sits, hunched, sprawling or occasionally straight-backed at his work, and each seems to be engulfed in a hill of paper. Wherever you look, everywhere across that nightmare floor, there are heaps, wodges, stacks of paper – paper tied in huge bundles, paper stuffed into sockets, paper spread out on desktops, or cluttered in trays, or strewn across the floor, and through it all the bureaucracy seems to be impotently floundering. The room is in a condition of sluggish diligence. Typewriters clack somewhere, occasionally a telephone rings, girls move unhurriedly up and down those tattered ranks, collecting dockets or returning files, waiters in stained white jackets dispense Turkish coffee and glasses of water from silver-plated trays, and ever through the tubes above one can hear the message cylinders, rattling across the intersections towards some unimaginable clearing centre out of sight.

'May I help you?' asks a peripatetic supervisor, carrying a large and battered clipboard.

'We are looking for the Department of Temporary Contributions.'

'Ah, that will be our Monsieur Tarbat, let me see now, Section A10 I believe' – he consults his board – 'ah no, he has passed to Section K . . . it must be – let me see – I think perhaps it's a branch of Domestic Registrations . . . I wonder now – patience, *mesdames*, forgive me –'

But at that moment we catch sight of our friend Boris, a keen member of the New Hav Film Society, accepting a coffee from a passing waiter. 'Temporary Contributions?' he laughs. 'Forget it, nobody has bothered about them since the end of the concessions. Put it out of your minds – enjoy yourselves!'

'Excellent advice,' says the supervisor, moving on.

Behind the Serai, in a ceremonious half-circle, stand the former legations. These were built on the edge of the old parade ground when the Russians first opened Hav to diplomatic representation, and are now given over to less lofty purposes, the British consul (who is called the Agent, actually) living at the former British Residency above the harbour. The legations are like a little museum of lost consequence, so many of their proud sponsors having vanished with the great convulsion of the First World War, but they are also a display of *fin de siècle* architectural styles. Thus the French built theirs, now the Hav Academy of Music and Dancing, in a sprightly Art Nouveau style, rich in coloured glass and ornamental lamp brackets, while the Americans next door erected one of the earliest steel-construction buildings in Europe – a building which, though now turned into the somewhat disconsolate Hav Museum, still looks by Hav standards remarkably up-to-date. My own favourite, though, is the wonderfully eccentric mansion at the northern end of the crescent, which is built partly of wood and partly of massive rusticated stone, and is splendidly embellished with balconies, external staircases, decorative busts, half-timbering and twisted chimney-pots in a style I can only describe as thoroughly Balkanesque. This was the legation of the Montenegrins, during the short-lived monarchy of the Black Mountain.

Nicholas I, the one and only king of Montenegro, had close links with Russian Hav. Two of his daughters married Russian Grand Dukes, he was an honorary Field-Marshal of the Imperial Army, and his Ruritanian capital of Cetinje was modelled upon the arrangements of the Czars. Every year, when the Russian aristocracy descended upon the peninsula by train from the north, Nicholas was disembarked upon its shores from the south, having sailed there in state on board the royal yacht *Petar Njegoš*. In the years before Sarajevo he was one of Hav's most familiar celebrities, contributing to all charities, attending all summer balls, gracing every garden party, sitting through every ballet and even having a street named in his honour – the Boulevard de Cetinje, an entirely unnecessary but properly dignified thoroughfare which the Russians cut through the Medina in 1904 in order to reach their bathing station beyond the western hills.

It was not surprising that when the Russians invited specified powers to open legations in Hav, the Montenegrins were among the first to accept. No conceivable diplomatic interest required the representation of the Black Mountain in this inessential station, but the King welcomed the chance to build himself a villa in such a prime position, within the Forbidden City so to speak. The legation is generally claimed to be a replica of his own palace at Cetinje, but it is really no more than an idealized approximation, being, as it happens, rather bigger and much more comfortable.

At eleven every morning the guard changes outside the Serai. This is an engaging spectacle. Since the departure of the Russians the gubernatorial guards have always been Circassians, recruited in Turkey. They are a stalwart crew, and provide solaces of many kinds, so the common rumour says, for both the wives of high officials, and the high officials themselves. Their pageantry is fine. They move less like soldiers than stage performers, in a flourishing, curly style, marching to a modified goose-step, swinging their arms exaggerat-edly, and wearing upon their faces stylized smiles of ingratiation, or perhaps self-satisfaction. Their orders I take to be shouted in Circassian, since nobody I have met understands a syllable of them, and they are armed with rifles inherited from the Russians for which there is, I am assured, no longer any ammunition.

No matter: the ceremonial life of the Serai is essentially easy-going anyway. The old protocol of the Russians has been whittled away, rule by rule, precedent by precedent down the years, and the nearest the Governor comes to any kind of grand-ducal progress nowadays is an occasional outing in his official barouche to pay a call upon the leader of one community or another. Then the guard lines up to see him off, smiling indefatigably, and the barouche is followed out of the palace yard, across the avenue of palms, by a pair of jolly postilions wearing their astrakhan hats at a jaunty angle and equipped with gleaming swords.

But there, even in Hav, all is not picturesque flummery around the seat of power. Even the lovable Serai, it seems, has its anxieties. As it happened when I was walking across the square one morning last week the Governor did come clopping out in his carriage, hauled by four high-stepping but rather shaggy greys, and followed by those stagy postilions. The guard saluted them as they passed, and they turned to the right, down the narrow street beside the South Block in the direction of the Medina. Hardly had they gone, however, than I heard a commotion of shouting and counter-shouting. I ran to the corner at once, and was in time to see one of the postilions, dismounted, thwacking a young man over the shoulders brutally with the flat of his sword. The youth slid to his haunches against the wall, his hands over his head. The postilion agilely remounted and cantered after the disappearing cortège.

I ran to the spot as fast as I could, and the young man looked up at me with a gaunt and melancholy face. 'What's happening?' I cried. 'Are you all right?' But he answered me – how disconcerting! – with a spit.

APRIL

Hav Rig

5

Immediately outside my window is the circular Place des Nations, supervised by a large statue of Count Alexander Kolchok, the last and most famous of the Russian Governors. It was erected, so the plinth says, 'IN HOMAGE', by the administrators of the Tripartite Mandate, and shows him in court dress, loaded with medals and holding a scroll. Very proper, because if it were not for Kolchok there would have been no mandate, and no Place des Nations either.

Lenin never came to Hav, so far as is known (though a film made by Soviet dissidents is supposed to show him shamelessly dissipated among the flesh-pots). When in 1917 the news of the Revolution reached Russian Hav, which had been a demilitarized zone throughout the First World War, Kolchok the governor immediately declared the place a White Russian republic, and called for help from the Western Allies. A French brigade was sent from Salonika, and Hav remained in a kind of limbo until in 1924 the League of Nations declared its mandate over the peninsula, and appointed Kolchok, the last governor under the old dispensation, the first governor under the new. He it was who, until his death in 1931 (he is buried here), presided over the unique experiment in international reconciliation which was Hav between the wars.

The delegates at Geneva invited three powers to take control of the peninsula, and to establish commercial concessions there: France because, so Magda would say, there was no choice – the French army was already on the spot, and unlikely to budge; Italy, because the Italians demanded parity with the French as a Mediterranean power; and in a stroke of unexampled idealism, the Weimar Republic of Germany, which was not then even a member of the League. Hav kept its old Russian forms of government, but with an elected instead of a nominated assembly; and across the harbour from the Medina there arose the international concessionary quarter of New Hav. It is in the very heart of this circular settlement that I have my apartment, looking down on the Place des Nations and the triumphant Count.

Actually he does not look *altogether* triumphant, because the open space around him, once so elegant, is now sadly run down, while he himself is patchy with verdigris and bird droppings. The formal gardens are overgrown and weedy, the railings sag, and as I look down now I see a couple of figures swathed in brown stretched out asleep upon the benches. Still, the statue remains the focal point of New Hav. A wide tree-lined ring road surrounds the Place des Nations, and from it run the three boulevards which divide the international quarter, Avenue de France, Viale Roma, and Unter den Südlinden – which is shaded in fact not by limes but by lovely Hav catalpas.

The grand plan of Hav was imposed by the League, but within each national segment, served by smaller streets, the concessionary powers could do as they liked. From the start, all three parts developed strong national characteristics, and even now I know almost without thinking, as I wander through New Hav, which quarter I am in. The smart restaurants, the fashion houses and the clubs have gone, to be replaced by Greek and Syrian stores, import–export agents, homelier eating houses and the offices of dubious investment banks; but it is the easiest thing in the world, early in the evening especially, when the cafés are filling up and the young people are strolling arm-in-arm beneath the shade of the trees towards the Lux Palace or the Cinema Malibran, to summon up New Hav in its brief but glittering heyday.

Here, for example, in some fusty drapers' shop I sense even now the charm of the boutique it used to be, and here a frieze of senators, helmeted soldiers and grateful Africans transports me instantly to Mussolini's Anno XIV. How earnest the peeling Gymnasium, with its busts of Goethe, Schubert and Beethoven! How sadly plush the Hotel Adler-Hav, with its velvet upholsteries, its gilt sofas and the tarnished mirrors of its Golden Bar, 'the longest bar on the Mediterranean'! The names of the streets, often the names of the shops too, still speak of other countries far away; and even today, though the faces you see around you are overwhelmingly Levantine, often you will hear blurred deviations of French, German or Italian along these nostalgic pavements.

And of course there are a few living survivors of the international regime, which lingered on increasingly inchoate until the abolition of the concessions in 1945. Of these the best-known is Armand Sauvignon the novelist, who came to Hav as a young attaché with the French administration in 1928, and wrote all his books here (his fictional Polova is really Hav). He is in his eighties now, a widower for twenty years, and lives amidst his large library in an apartment overlooking the French cathedral. He embodies in himself, as it were, the whole history of New Hav, start to finish, and talking to him is like reliving the whole brave but somehow unreal initiative, street by street, character by character. He has a long beaky nose, a creased brow, and an odd mannerism of pursing his mouth between sentences, and all these features combine to give his company a more or less continual irony.

His first job was to be French observer at the concessionary courts, which dealt with all cases involving nationals of the mandatory powers, but whose judges were appointed directly by the League. 'Such a collection, you can have no idea! It was like a music-hall. We had judges, I swear to you, who never saw a court of law before. The convenor would hiss at them "Twelve years", "Deport him", or "Insufficient evidence", and His Honour would gather his robes around him, put on his gravest face, and do what he was told. It was killing! We had a judge from Texas, I remember (you must realize Americans were not so worldly then), who used to bring his accordion with him to court, to entertain us between cases. In the evening it was the thing for us young attachés, the Italians, the Germans, ourselves – we were all good friends – to go out to the Palace of Delights in Yuan Wen Kuo; once after a particularly gruelling fraud case, I remember, hour after hour in the hot courts, we all went out there to relax, and who should we discover playing his accordion in the Hall of Fair Beauties but old Judge Bales, surrounded by girls and half-incoherent with opium!'

'You seem to have lived merry old lives.'

'In the early years, very merry. Things changed later, as the world changed. But when New Hav was really new we were intoxicated by it all. You must remember the Great War had not long ended, we were lucky to be alive at all, and here we were working together in this place almost as though our peoples had never been enemies.

'Besides, in the twenties and thirties Hav was extremely smart. My Polova was no exaggeration. The Russian aristocrats were still in their villas here, living on the last of their jewels and ikons, and when the Casino was opened, about 1927 I think it was, anybody who had a steam-yacht in the Mediterranean came to Hav sooner or later. People used to take the train from Paris to Moscow especially to catch the Mediterranean Express down here – you should talk to the tunnel pilots, they have amazing things to recall.

'You see that poor old hotel there, the Bristol? It doesn't look much now, does it, but believe me it was as smart as any hotel in Europe for a few years. Noël Coward wrote most of *Pastiche* there, did you know? I met him at the Agency one evening, a tiresome person I thought him. Hemingway used to go there too – they will still mix you a very nasty cocktail called Papa's Sting, I believe . . .

'All the great performers came. Goodman, Chevalier, the Hot Club de France. We met them all. My first chief here was a very great swell, the Marquis de Chablon, and he virtually set up a court at our Residency. The Germans and the Italians had nobody so *soigné*, the governors after Kolchok were nonentities, so really the social whirl of Hav revolved around us. For a young man, and especially a young artist, it was a dream. Out of season we had to find our own pleasures – shooting on the escarpment, pony-racing, the Palace of Delights of course. But in the summer, my God! we lived like millionaires!'

We were strolling as we talked, in the warm of the evening, among the straggly press of the boulevards, and their mingled smells of food, dirt, jasmine and imperfectly refined gasoline. We had walked all through the Italian quarter, and down past the Schiller Fountain (in whose water ugly fat carp swam in the half-light – 'like submarines,' said Sauvignon. 'Don't you think so? Yellow submarines') and we were in his own territory now, on the pavement opposite the Bristol. He took my arm. 'You have half an hour?' he said. 'Join me in an aperitif – and a glimpse of the past.'

We passed through the huge dark foyer, where an old porter rose to his feet as Sauvignon passed by, and a clerk behind the reception desk, in open-necked pale blue shirt and gold necklace, murmured a greeting; we passed the almost empty dining-room, decorated with large now-brownish murals of Parisian life; and pushing open a brass-handled double door inlaid with figures of seahorses and mermaids, we entered the Bar 1924. It was absolutely packed. Every table was full, but an obliging waiter, recognizing my companion, squeezed a party of young Lebanese together and found room for us. The air was full of Turkish tobacco smoke; the waiter thrust before us a stained typewritten list of archaic cocktails – Sledgehammers, Riproarers, Topper's Special, and yes, Papa's Sting! Blaring above it all, deafeningly vigorous and brassy, there was jazz.

It was an elderly combo which, spotting Sauvignon through the haze, dipped its instruments in welcome: a grizzled black trumpeter, a trombonist with rimless spectacles, a gentlemanly Chinese pianist, a grey-beard playing bass and a middle-aged elf in a red shirt frenzied at the drums. They performed with a somewhat desperate enthusiasm, I thought, a repertoire of long ago. Sometimes somebody shouted a request – 'Honeysuckle Rose!' 'A-Train!' 'Sentimental Journey!' The pianist had a small cup of coffee on his piano. The trumpeter occasionally groaned 'Yeah man . . .', but more in duty than in ecstasy. 'Yellow Submarine!' called Sauvignon during a pause in the music, and as the trombonist broke into an approximate lyric – *'Weallivinayellersummerine'* – he raised his Manhattan towards me in a toast. 'To yesterday's youth,' he said.

Above the door of No. 24 Residenzstrasse in the old German quarter, hardly a stone's throw across the Viale Roma from my apartment, there is a modern plaque in German. It commemorates the fact that between 1941 and 1945 members of the German anti-Nazi resistance movement, *der Widerstand*, were given refuge there under the clandestine protection of the German concessionary administration.

The development of New Hav, and its last apotheosis during the Second World War, was as extraordinary as its beginning. Isolated there on that distant foreshore, with poor communications and the loosest of supervision from Geneva, the three regimes developed almost autonomously. The Italians, who saw themselves from the start as colonists, threw themselves enthusiastically into Mussolini's imperial designs, putting up *fasces* all over the place, erecting ostentatious murals depicting Mare Nostrum or Africa Revicta, proudly welcoming Marshal de Bono when he paid a visit after his conquest of Ethiopia, and eventually refusing even to receive the timid representatives of collective security who now and then arrived on the train from Switzerland. They had high hopes, Signora Vattani has confided in me (her husband, she claims, was an 'important official' in the administration) – they had high hopes of taking over the whole of Hav, if ever war gave them a chance, and when war did come they openly disregarded the laws of neutrality by re-provisioning Italian submarines in the harbour.

The French treated Hav above all as a place of pleasure and prestige. They wished their quarter of New Hav to be a showcase of French panache. They sent stylish magnificos to be their Residents, the smartest young men of family to be their administrators. They sponsored visits by eminent musicians and French drama companies. The French gracefully gave way to their partners when it came to matters of political priority or protocol, but they saw to it that their quarter was much the most inviting, and made sure that, as Armand Sauvignon says, the social life of Hav revolved around their handsomely Moorish-style Residency on its artificial hillock. When France fell to the Germans in 1940 the Resident of the day, the ineffably fashionable Guyot de Delvert, unhesitatingly declared for Vichy, had banners portraying Marshal Pétain flying all down the Rue de France, and no longer sent social invitations to the British Agency.

The Germans' was the oddest role. 'Those Boches,' Sauvignon told me once, 'really, to a well-brought-up young man direct from the Sorbonne, they were like people from another planet.' Subjects as they were of liberal Weimar, they set out to make their quarter of New Hav its properly representative outpost. 'You would never have believed it! You could do anything over there, you could assume any personality you pleased. I never saw such cabarets – even the Egyptians were shocked sometimes. The place was full of drug-addicts, poets, homosexuals, pacifists, God knows what – everyone you met was writing a novel. I used to go over there to the Café München whenever I felt the pressures of social life too great for me, and I was sure to find myself in a group of writers or artists, some actually from Germany, but Turks too, and Syrians, and really people from everywhere. I met Thomas Mann there once. He asked me what was the right way to pronounce *mésalliance*, I remember . . .'

I constantly hear astonishing stories about the behaviour of the German diplomats during the Second World War. Signora Vattani thought it traitorous – 'they should all have been shot, if you ask me.' Others thought it truly heroic. There were only two German Residents during the entire history of New Hav, and they both stood firmly in the German liberal tradition. The second of them, Heinrich von Tranter, was appointed to office in 1932, the year before Hitler came to power. By guile and social influence, and some say by the connivance of von Papen, the impenetrable German Ambassador in Ankara, he managed to hang on to his post throughout the Second World War, and made Hav a secret refuge and headquarters for Germans opposed to the Nazi regime.

'We knew nothing,' Signora V. fervently assures me. 'We had no idea what was going on. Do you think we would have allowed it, endangering our own men and ships? Why those ruffians were in daily touch with the British Agent, giving him all sorts of information all the time!'

But had not Fatima Yeğen told me that Hitler himself was supposed to have visited Hav during the war?

'He did, he did, he came down incognito in a special car on the train with that von Papen. We knew nothing of it, we had no idea, and then on the Tuesday morning I was crossing Unter den Südlinden to get some sausages at the German delicatessen – they had excellent sausages throughout the war – and I looked up and there was von Tranter's big black car coming slowly down the boulevard, and a motor-cycle escort all around it, and who should be sitting in it but Hitler himself, with von Tranter beside him and von Papen sitting in the front with the driver. I was never so astonished. Look, I was saying to everyone on the pavement, look, it's Herr Hitler! but half of them didn't believe it even when they saw him for themselves. The very next morning he was gone again, they say. We were told a U-boat picked him up at Malaya Yalta and took him to Italy.'

Yet even Hitler, if he really did come (and if you believe that, in my opinion, you will believe anything), even Hitler apparently did not suspect what was going on under the aegis of his own swastika at 24 Residenzstrasse. Throughout the later years of the war a steady stream of German dissidents and resistance workers were smuggled through Turkey or by sea to Hav, where they coordinated escapes and clandestine missions secret even now. It was perfectly true, as Signora Vattani so scornfully alleges, that von Tranter was in touch with the British in Hav: this was a main point of contact between the German underground and the Western Allies. If the Fascists of the Italian quarter did not know what was going on across the Viale Roma, the British secret service certainly did, and time and again its agents and interrogators came into Hav by submarine from Cyprus and Egypt.

To many people these wartime conspiracies were the ultimate justification for the whole experiment of New Hav, but the German quarter was to acquire an ironic new reputation later. Von Tranter survived the war but died in mysterious circumstances at his home near Augsburg in 1947, and when the concessions came to an end Germans of a very different kind moved into Hav, well-fed, muscular men of undisclosed resources, with their stalwart wives and some-times lissom mistresses. They kept themselves as closely to them-selves as had von Tranter's hidden wards, living communally in the vacated villas of Russian noblemen, guarded by burly bodyguards behind wire fences. They were, it is said, members of Odessa, the clandestine organization of former SS officers, and through Hav they are supposed to have channelled immense illegal funds, arranged the disappearances of criminal colleagues, and organized fraternal net-works throughout the world.

I am assured they have nearly all gone now – most of them are dead – but when Armand and I were walking one evening along the harbourside promenade of New Hav we were passed by a bent and slender elderly man of thoughtful appearance in a well-cut tweed suit and a felt hat. He bowed slightly to Sauvignon, and the Frenchman raised his hat in return. 'You see that old man?' said my companion when we were out of earshot. 'There are people in Israel who would give a million francs to discover his whereabouts.'

'You're never tempted?' I asked.

'No, my dear. If there is one thing I have learnt from Hav, it is the uselessness of revenge. To be alive is punishment enough for that old ogre.'

6

Spring – flora and fauna – the Kretevs – the day of the snow raspberry – my yellow hat

Away beyond the Serai domes one can see the outlines of the western hills, where the Greeks built their pleasure-houses (so archaeologists assure us) and the Russians after them. When I came to this apartment they looked brown and melancholy, like so much else in Hav. Then, almost as I watched, they became perceptibly greener and happier. And yesterday, when I went out on to my balcony with my morning coffee, lo! they were a magical blush of pinks, blues and yellows.

'The spring of Hav!' announced Signora V emotionally. 'It is not,' she added, as she invariably adds, 'as it used to be' (in the Duce's day, I almost interjected), 'but still it is a kind of miracle. How wonderful nature is even in these distant places.'

I have acquired a car now. It is a 1971 Renault, and according to Fatima, who arranged the deal for me, it was once the tunnel pilot's transport. So in the afternoon I drove out to the hills to see the spring flowers for myself – swiftly through the wrinkled alleys of the Medina, along the fine big road the Russians built to take them to their pleasures, across the remains of the Spartan canal until the low hills rose on either side of me, speckled with neglected olive trees, decrepit villas and overgrown gardens. And the Signora was right: a miracle it was. Every patch of broken ground, every gulley, every broken-down Grand Duke's or Sturmbannführer's terrace was lyrically overlaid with flowers, half of them strange to me – flowers something like buttercups, but not quite, flowers very nearly bluebells, flowers not unrelated to asphodels or recognizably akin to primroses – and there were clambering plants with pink petals wandering everywhere, and up the gnarled trunks of the olive trees a sort of blossoming moss flourished. The combined scent of all these flowers, and many another herb, scrub and lichen no doubt, resolved itself into something peculiarly pungent, not unlike a sweet vinaigrette dressing, and overcome by this I lay out there flat on my back encouched in foliage. There was not a soul about. All those once-blithe houses, with their tattered awnings and their sagging pergolas, seemed to be utterly deserted. Far away over the canal the towers and gilded domes of Hav, the great grey-gold mass of the castle, looked from that bowered belvedere like a city of pure fiction.

It was absolutely silent there. I heard not a bird nor a cricket, was stung by no ant, bitten by no wandering gnat. Though Heaven knows Hav is no showplace of hygiene, I sometimes feel it to be almost antiseptically sterile. There seems to be a shortage of everyday bug, bird or rodent life. The other day I had lunch at the Athenaeum with Dr Borge, who likes to describe himself as Botanist, Anthropologist and Philosopher, and I put this point to him. 'You are right,' he said, as philosophers will, 'and you are wrong. You must realize that here in Hav our conditions of life are unusual. We are at once maritime and continental, Triassic and Jurassic, marsh and salt, lime and mud. Our fauna is not lavish, but as your Bard would say, it is true to ourselves!'

Such animal life as there is, sustained by this rare combination of soils, climates and geological origins, really is sufficiently peculiar. Once or twice in the greenery immediately below my balcony I have seen a strange little snouted creature snooping in the dusk, black, soft and low on the ground. This is the Hav mongoose, *Herpestes hav*, a mutation of the Indian mongoose brought in by the British to deal with the snakes; there is a stuffed specimen in the museum's little zoological collection, and it looks to me less like a mongoose than a kind of furry anteater.

Then the Hav hedgehog, *Erinaceus hav*, is odd too, since it is tailed, like a prickly armadillo, and the Hav terrier is like a little grey ball of wire wool, and I believe the troglodytes breed a pony of Mongolian origins on the foot-slopes of the escarpment. Some people say the so-called Abyssinian cat, now so fashionable in Europe and America, really came from Hav, in the kitbags of British soldiers; as it happened, the British garrison here was closed in the same year as the 1868 expedition to Magdala in Ethiopia, and it is suggested that some sharp characters among the returning soldiery conceived the idea of putting a new 'rare African cat' on the market. The modern Hav cat does not look much like the slinky patricians of Western fancy, but he is often distinguished by having extra claws on his front paws – the extra-toed cats which still swarm about Ernest Hemingway's house in Key West are claimed to have Hav ancestry.

Out on the marshes there are sheep, guarded by hangdog Arab shepherds (and hangdog they might well be, there in those dismal wastes). They are dull stringy creatures, but around them there often romp and scamper, as though in a state of permanent hilarious mockery, lithe and fleecy goats – so tirelessly jerky, springy and enterprising that from a distance, when you see one of those listless flocks like a stain on the flatlands, the goats prancing around it look like so many little devils.

I don't know what the British Resident's original cattle were like, when they arrived from England on the frigate *Octavia* in 1821, but the Hav cattle of today, who are all their descendants, would win no rosettes at county shows. Disconsolately munching the scrubby turf in their pastures at the foot of the escarpment, they seem to have gone badly to seed, having long pinched faces, heavy haunches and protruding midriffs. They have never been crossed with any other cattle, Dr Borge tells me, but I suspect the poor wizened cows among them would welcome the arrival, on some later *Octavia* perhaps, of a few lusty newcomers.

There are foxes, they say, on the escarpment. There are certainly rabbits. There used to be wolves; the last of them, allegedly shot by Count Kolchok himself on 4 June 1907, is mounted in the entrance hall of the Serai's North Block, looking a bit the worse for death. And only the other day, I read in *La Gazette*, a member of the Hav Zoological Society claimed to have spotted, while snake-hunting on the escarpment (where the mongoose never did thrive) a female Hav bear.

This rarest of European bears (*Ursus arctus hav*), which looks from pictures rather like a miniature grizzly, has repeatedly been declared extinct. Hunting the survivors was one of the fashionable pastimes of the *fin de siècle*: the King of Montenegro shot three or four, and you may see the skin of one still hanging in his wooden palace at home in Cetinje. As late as the 1930s, though the Tripartite Government had declared the animals protected, hunting parties used to go out from the Casino equipped with all the paraphernalia of safari, and sometimes claimed to have shot one: it was during one of these expeditions that Hemingway, so legend says, deliberately jogged the elbow of Count Ciano, thus saving the life of a bear offering a perfect shot upon the skyline ('You fool,' said the Count. 'You fascist,' said the writer).

Anyway, the bear apparently survives, nobody is quite sure how. The terrain of the escarpment is difficult and infertile, yet *Ursus arctus hav* has never, it seems, wandered over the crest into the easier flatlands of Anatolia, and has rarely been sighted in the Hav lowlands either. There were reports in the 1950s that a covey had somehow made themselves a lair within the escarpment tunnel – maintenance men reported seeing animal eyes glowing in alcoves as they went by on their trollies, and for a time amateur zoologists went backwards and forwards on the train, to and from the frontier station, unavailingly hoping to catch a glimpse of them. More persistently, rumour has the Kretevs sheltering the bear in their warren of caves at the western end of the escarpment, either because they believe it to be holy, or just because they are fond of it. 'The troglodytes,' Dr Borge told me learnedly, 'possess a special relationship with the animal world, not unlike I believe that of the ancient Minoans. You are aware of the Minoans? They venerated a monster, you will remember, within a labyrinth. Perhaps our Kretevs cherish other creatures within their caves?' It seemed improbable, I suggested, that only thirty-odd miles from the cafeteria of the Athenaeum such mysteries could persist. 'Ah,' said the young doctor, 'but you have not met the troglodytes. You do not know their obstinacy.'

Actually I have met some of them – I cultivate their acquaintance at the morning market, and have even struck up a sort of friendship with one of their more articulate stall-holders, who learnt some English as a merchant seaman, and whose name sounds to me like Brack. I concede, though, that of all the manifestations of nature in

Hav, the Kretevs seem the most elusive. Talking the arcane unwritten language which, it is said, no foreign adult has ever mastered, crouched over their stalls with long tangled hair often half-bleached by the sun, their nondescript clothes set off by many bracelets and ear-rings, down at the market they seem to me like a race of gypsy Rastafarians, visiting the town from some other country altogether. Even Brack claims never to have set foot within the circuit of New Hav.

Yet they form a still living bridge between the city and its remotest origins. In the second or first centuries before Christ, the theory is, Celts from the Anatolian interior found their way to the edge of the great escarpment and saw before them, probably for the first time in their lives, the sea. So blue it seemed, we are told, so warm was the Mediterranean prospect, that they called the place simply 'Summer' – still *hav* or *haf* in the surviving Celtic languages of the West, just as 'Kretev' is thought to be etymologically related to the Welsh *crwydwyr*, wanderers. They were a continental people, though, a people of the land mass, and they never did settle upon the peninsula proper, forming instead troglodytic colonies in the raddled limestone caverns where their descendants still live. Their fellow-Celts of the interior presently evolved into the Galatians; and it was the poor Kretevs that St Paul had in mind when he wrote in his Epistle to the Galatians of 'your ignorant brethren living like conies in the rocks of the south'.

They are like strange familiars of the peninsula, and on one day in the year they perform a truly magical or mythological service to the city of Hav, whose foundation their presence here so long preceded, and from whose affairs they remain so generally remote. At dawn one morning, usually near the beginning of February, their gaily decorated pick-ups come storming into the morning market with far more than their usual gusto, blowing their horns fit to wake the Governor and out-blast Missakian's trumpet. They are not unexpected, since it happens every year, and the market throws itself immediately *en fête*. Every truck horn blows, every ship's siren hoots, and all the market people line the street to greet them. They are bringing, or rather one of the trucks is bringing, the first of the snow raspberries.

Almost the last too, for this supreme delicacy is to be found only on three or four days of the year, when the early spring suns melt the last of the escarpment's winter snows. Like the dragon-fly, the snow raspberry is born only to die. It sprouts mushroom-like overnight, without warning, and by noonday it is gone. It grows only in shaded crannies of the limestone, and only the cave people know where to look for it, or are there to pick it anyway. Brack says he was first taken out to gather the snow raspberries when he was five years old.

The arrival of this fruit in Hav is like the arrival of the first Beaujolais Nouveau in Paris, or the first grouse of the season in London, but much more exciting than either. Nobody knows just when the snow raspberry will appear, and for a week or two around the end of January the morning market, they tell me, is in a high state of expectancy. Even Signor Biancheri has no prior claim to supplies – even he must await the day when, honking their celebratory way past the sleeping city, the troglodytes arrive in wild array with their small but priceless commodity. The cost of snow raspberries is phenomenal. Few people in Hav have ever tasted the fruit, and nobody outside Hav has ever tasted it at all, for if it is frozen it loses its savour altogether. I suppose the Kretevs themselves may eat a few, but otherwise almost every berry goes to the government (official receptions of the most important kind are often timed to coincide with the snow raspberry season), to Biancheri's kitchen at the Casino, or to the Chinese millionaires of Yuan Wen Kuo.

Signora Vattani claims to have tasted one in her youth, but I don't believe her for a moment. Fatima Yeğen says that the Kaiser, who was lucky enough to arrive in Hav at just the right moment, was given a basket of them to eat on his ride down the Staircase. Dr Borge claims to believe them imaginary – 'folk-loric, nothing more' – and says the Kaiser was probably palmed off with Syrian loganberries. But Armand ate one once, on 8 February 1929, when an international delegation from the League of Nations was feted at the Palace.

'Oh it was so funny, how you would have laughed! In came this single footman, as pompous as a monsignor, carrying a silver dish piled high with these snow raspberries. The biggest ones were on the top. I was just a young attaché, at the foot of the table almost. All down the room I heard the oohs and aahs, "wonderful", "*quelle expérience*", you know the kind of thing. But by the time the dish reached us young people at the end of the room, only a few shrivelled little red fruits remained for us. They tasted like very old dry cherries.

'My dear, you must not be shocked. We were very young and disrespectful. My dear friend Ulrich Helpmann, from the German Residency, who was the most disrespectful of us all, placed his precious raspberry on the palm of his hand and flicked it with his right forefinger – so! – across the table at me. It missed me altogether and hit the boiled shirt of the footman standing behind my chair. I mean to say, my dear, before you could blink your eye that man had scooped it off and eaten it. His one and only snow raspberry! He's probably boasting of it still.'

Anyway, as I was saying, spring is here. The shuttered colourless Hav that greeted me has disappeared. The flowers are blooming in the western hills, and everything else is tentatively blooming too. Even the functionaries of the Serai, when I went to have my permit stamped this morning, were emancipated into shirtsleeves. The sentries at the Palace are in white uniforms now, with smashing gold epaulettes, and the station café has set up its pavement tables on the edge of Pendeh Square, under the palms, beneath well-patched blue, white and green sunshades. I wore my yellow towelling hat from Australia to go to the Serai. *'Başında kavak yelleri esiyor,'* a passer-by said without pausing, which translated from the Hav Turkish means 'There is the springtime in your hat!'

7

The Arabs – A Muslim city – the 125th Caliph – 'you seem surprised' – Olga Naratlova – not so peaceful – Hav 001 – salt

I can hear the call to prayer only faintly in the mornings. Though it is electrically amplified, from the minaret of the mosque of Malik, the Grand Mosque in the Medina, it is not harshly distorted, as it is so often in Arab countries, but remains fragile and other-worldly; what is more it is not recorded, but really is sung every morning by the muezzin who climbs the precipitous eleventh-century staircase of the minaret. For me it is much the most beautiful sound in Hav: just as for my taste the Arab presence in this city remains the most haunting – more profound than the Russian flamboyances, more lasting than the hopes of New Hav, less aloof than the Chinese ambience, more subtle than the Turkish . . .

Besides, though the massive structures of the Serai may seem dominant when you first arrive in Pendeh Square, gradually you come to realize that it was the Arabs who really created this city. They gave it its great days, its glory days. Although for more than a century they were supplanted by the Crusaders, in effect they dominated Hav for four hundred years, and they made it rich. Through Hav half the spices, skins, carpets, works of art and learning of the Muslim East found their way into Europe – and not only the Muslim East, for this sophisticated and well-equipped mart between the sea and the land, between Asia and Europe, became the chief staging-post of the Silk Route from the further Orient. Ibn Batuta, in the fourteenth century, called it one of the six greatest ports of the world, the others being Alexandria in Egypt, Quilon and

Calicut in India, Sudaq in the Crimea and Zaitun in China. Here the Venetians established their Fondaco di Cina, their China Warehouse, and here later the very first Chinese colony of the west settled itself in the peninsula known to the Arabs as Yuan Wen Kuo, Land of the Distant Warmth. Great was the fame of Arab Hav, attested by many an old traveller, and its last splendours were extinguished only when in 1460 the Ottoman Turks, deposing the last of the Hav Amirs and expelling the Venetians, incorporated the peninsula into their own domains and so plunged it, for nearly four centuries, into the dispirited gloom of their despotism.

When the troops of the Seljuks first arrived in Hav in 1079 they must have thought it a sorry sort of conquest. It had never come to much before – had never remotely rivalled the powerful city-states of the Asia Minor shore, Seleucia, Smyrna, Trebizond. Alexander had passed it by, both the Romans and the Persians had ignored it. By the time the Arabs got there the remaining Greek inhabitants were living in miserable squalor beside the harbour, their acropolis long since a ruin above them. The salt-flats were undrained then. Malaria was endemic. There was no road up the escarpment and the Kretevs were unapproachable. Yet here the Arabs built the northernmost of their great trading cities, and most of it is still to be seen.

To the north of the castle hill they established quarters for their slaves – obdurate infidels and prisoners-of-war – and these were to develop into the wan suburbs of the Balad. To the west they built their own walled headquarters, and this is now the Old City, or Medina. The huge public place they laid out was the progenitor of today's Pendeh Square, and the second of their great mosques, erected by Saladin after his liberation of Hav from the Crusaders, now does service as the Greek Orthodox cathedral, behind the railway station. The Staircase up the escarpment was first cut by Arab engineers, and it was they who drained the salt-marshes.

It is all there still, and above all the Medina remains, even now, overwhelmingly an Arab medieval city. It is crudely intersected by the Boulevard de Cetinje, but is still a glorious jumble of alleys and sudden squares, alive with the sights and sounds of Araby – you know, the dark and the sunshine of it, the shuffle and the beat, the sour hoof-smell from the smithy, the towering simplicity of the mosque in the heart of it all – you know, you know!

For some Muslims, if only a lingering few, that mosque is one of the holiest on earth, because a small and dwindling sect claims it to be the shrine of the Caliphate. You will remember that the Ottoman sultans, whose temporal powers were abolished in 1924, claimed also to be the legitimate caliphs of Islam, the spiritual leaders of the faith. They were recognized as such by many Muslims of the Sunni persuasion, and even after the extinction of their sultanate, proclaimed themselves caliphs still. The deposed Mehmet V tried to establish himself in the Holy Land of the Hejaz itself, his cousin Abdulmecid maintained the claim from Paris until his death there in 1944, and a contemporary aspirant to the Caliphate, Namik Abdulhamid, who says he is 125th in the true line of descent from Abu Bakr, the Prophet's father-in-law, lives in Hav, the nearest he can get to the Turkey from which the Sultan's dynasty and all its pretenders have been permanently exiled. Yesterday I had an audience with him.

This had taken time to achieve. The 125th Caliph lives cautiously. I had a letter of introduction to him, from a man in Cairo whose name I should not mention, in case somebody assassinates him; and finding it difficult to discover just where the Caliph resided, this I presented to the Imam at the Grand Mosque. For a week or two there was no response. Then one evening an excited Signora Vattani told me there had been a call, good gracious Signora Morris, a call from the Caliphate! I was to be ready to be picked up at the apartment the following evening, five o'clock sharp. But five o'clock came and went without a sign, and next day I was told, without apologies, to be ready that night instead. Twice more I waited, twice more no caliphian car arrived; it was only on the fourth evening that, exactly at five as the man on the telephone had said, the doorbell rang and a big black American car, of the fin-and-chrome era, awaited me outside.

There was a chauffeur in Arab dress, but the car's back door opened from the inside, and there sat a dapper middle-aged man in a black suit, sun-glasses and that almost forgotten badge of Ottoman respectability, a tarboosh. 'A tarboosh!' I could not stop myself exclaiming '– can you still buy them?' 'The Caliph has his own supplier, in Alexandria – Tadros Nakhla and Sons, you may perhaps know the name? Very old-established.'

He introduced himself as the Caliph's Wazir, and as we drove across the square he apologized for the inconveniences of the past three days. I would understand, he was sure. The Caliph was vulnerable. One had to be careful. It seemed an inadequate excuse to me, but I let it pass, and the Wazir went on to explain that because of certain, well, entanglements of a historical nature the 125th Caliph found it necessary to live in the strictest security – all through history, he reminded me, the Caliphate had been an office of the greatest delicacy – I would recall what happened to Omar in the mosque at Kufa!

Down the Boulevard de Cetinje we sped, and out of the Old City, and before we reached the canal we turned up a gravel track, shaded by tall eucalyptus trees. 'People say,' remarked the Wazir, 'that this house was built for Count Kolchok's mistress, the lovely dancer Olga Naratlova. True? False?' He shrugged his neat shoulders. 'It makes a nice little story. The Caliph likes the fancy.' It looked an imposing love-nest, as we passed through lavishly ornamental gates, crossed a wide yard, and were debouched upon a portico whose doors were instantly opened by two swarthy men in khaki drill, one each side ('Assyrians,' the Wazir said breezily as we entered, as though they were deaf mutes). Through a bare but still luxurious hall . . . down a marbled corridor . . . two more Assyrians at a double door . . . and there rising courteously to greet me from a silken sofa was Nadik Abdulhamid.

He wore a red tarboosh too, and a suit of exquisite pale linen, and shoes that looked like lizardskin, and he held in his left hand a string of ivory prayer-beads, and in his right a cigarette in a long holder. He was clean-shaven, with heavy blue eyes and a becoming tan. All in all the pretender to the Caliphate was very suave, and not I thought very caliph-like, and he gestured me suavely to the sofa, and suavely offered me a cigarette from a silver box engraved in Arabic, and most suavely, as we talked, flicked his own ash into what looked like a solid gold ashtray.

'You seem surprised. I am not what you expected? Tell me frankly, what did you expect?'

Someone blackly bearded, I said, and sage, and dressed in the robes of holiness.

'Then you would have been perfectly satisfied with my father. He was all that! Nobody was much sager than my father! But I decided long ago that I would be myself. As you would say, the world must take me or leave me.'

And did not this worldly persona make him enemies?

'Oh yes, I should say so. Imagine what they think of me in Iran, or even in Saudi Arabia! They hate me very much. Do you know that I have never been allowed to make the holy pilgrimage to Mecca? If I went there they would tear me limb from limb.'

Coffee arrived, flavoured with camomile, together with biscuits on little scallop-edged plates, and the Caliph asked if I would like to see something of the house.

'You know its history, I dare say? Count Kolchok built it for his mistress, the dancer Olga Naratlova, who came to Hav with Diaghilev. Everything was taken from the house when Kolchok died, but I have had her portrait painted *in memoriam*' – and he showed me on the wall above our sofa a large and sickly representation, doubtless taken from a photograph, of a dark turn-of-the-century beauty, full length, leaning in a dress of satiny red against a truncated column.

'What became of her?'

'Ah, you must ask the Bolsheviks. She went home to Russia in 1918, and was never heard of again.'

Poor Olga. She sounds a lonely figure, hidden away here in such secluded luxury, and she is lonely still, for hers is the only portrait in the whole of the Caliph's house – 'and just think what the *Ikhwan* would say, if they knew I had *her*!' Otherwise the house, or as much as I saw of it, was severely undecorated. Spindly gilded armchairs and sofas were the nearest it got to creature comfort, unless you count the elaborate television, video and hi-fi equipment which the Caliph kept in his private sitting-room ('You may not be aware of it, but the Caliphate is a principal shareholder in Hav TV, so it is necessary for me to keep in touch . . .').

On we went, among the grand, beautifully kept but still desolate rooms, through the office where two male secretaries sat surrounded by files and typewriters with a telex in the corner; we were bowed to here and there by silent Assyrians, interrupted once by the Wazir for a brief reminder about that evening's later arrangements ('a most excellent fellow,' said the Caliph. 'Did you like him? He would make a fine husband for you') until on the terrace at the back of the house we stood before the small octagonal mosque, a marble miniature of the Dome of the Rock, which the Caliph had built, he told me, for his private use.

Two more Assyrians guarded it. 'I dare say you are also surprised,' said the Caliph, 'to find all these Assyrians. They are new to the Caliphate. I recruit them in Iraq, where as you may know for some generations they served the British military authorities, guarding camps, airfields and so forth. They are Christians, you see, with no particular allegiance to any state or power, and so very suitable to our needs. You must realize, Miss Morris, that my situation is precarious. Many people hate me, many people wish to use me.'

While the Western powers took no notice of him, he said, the Communists courted him. He had been to Moscow several times. He had many followers in Bokhara, Tashkent, and more recently in Kabul. 'You may perhaps have seen my picture at the May Day parade in Red Square in 1983? The late Mr Andropov was always especially good to me.' As for the Muslims of the Middle East, some of them loathed him, some would die for him, he claimed. 'The Iranians have twice tried to have me killed, once with a bomb in an aeroplane when I was travelling in Egypt, once here in this very house, with a gunman in the garden – you see, there are the bullet-holes still! Not everything in Hav, you know, is as peaceful as it seems. When you have been here a little longer you will come to realize that.'

And the Turks? The Caliph smiled a knowing and even more suave smile. 'The Turks will not allow me over that escarpment' – and he pointed through the trees to the distant dim line of the northern hills. 'I am a non-person to the Turks. And yet you know, Miss Morris, between ourselves – off the record, as they say – traditionally caliphs have been adept at travelling incognito, and so it is with me. I have been over that escarpment many times. I have many, many friends in my forebears' country. That is why they are afraid of me in Ankara, in Washington even – a flick of my finger, they think, and

I could start a revolution – as if I would want to! Even my sage father had no such plans.

'But still it is pleasant to go there now and then. How do I travel? Ah, that I cannot tell you. Suffice it to say that there are certain people not unconnected with the railway administration who have been for many generations faithful adherents of the Caliphate . . .'

Laughing heartily, conspiratorially and sophisticatedly, all at the same time, the Caliph called for an Assyrian to show me to the waiting car. 'You must remember, if you ever need anything, any help that the house of a caliph can afford, or if you wish to marry the Wazir after all, you are to telephone me at once. And now,' he concluded unexpectedly, 'you must allow me to excuse myself, for it is time for my evening prayers.' With a gentle bow, and a smile full of self-amusement, he disappeared inside his little sanctuary.

His telephone number is Hav OOI. I doubt if I shall ever ring it, but still my visit to Nadik Abdulhamid left me with a paradoxical sense of stability or at least of continuity. I have no idea how authentic is his claim to the Caliphate, and by his own account he leads a tricky kind of life, but there was something about his presence that made Hav feel still in the mainstream of Arab affairs, still in touch, however surreptitiously, with the debates, the feuds and the aspirations of Islam.

It is not all romantic illusion, either. Even today, they tell me, a remarkable proportion of Hav's Arabs have made the pilgrimage to Mecca, unlike the poor Caliph, and there is a regular flow of students to the University of Al Azhar in Cairo. Much the best-selling tapes at the Fantastique Video and Hi-Fi Shop in New Hav, so its manager tells me, are second-hand cassettes from Egypt, supplied by seamen from the salt ships.

The salt ships! I forgot to tell you! Today the strongest link of all between the Arabs of Hav and the Arabs of Arabia is the trade in Hav salt, whose wide sad pans I saw that first evening on the train. It is said to have been the Greeks who first discovered that salt extracted from the Hav marshes had aphrodisiac qualities: shiploads of it, they say, were sent to Attica, and according to Schliemann it was the salt that led Achilles to set up his base on Hav's western shore. By the Middle Ages the power of Hav's salt was so well-attested that some scholars think it was the first reason for the Arab seizure of the peninsula.

It was largely to work the salt-flats that the Arabs established that huge slave quarter, and when the Venetians struck up their commercial alliance with the Amirs salt became the staple of their triangular trade with the Egyptians. The great merchant convoys, assembling with their escorts off Crete, would sail first to Hav to ship salt, often having to fight terrible battles with the Turks along the way, then to Alexandria to exchange it for spices and ivories, before returning rich and glorious home.

After the expulsion of the Venetians the Arabs of Hav exported the salt themselves. By then it had long been prized, as it still is, all over the Muslim world. Ibn Batuta had tried it in Tunis as early as 1325, and was much impressed:

It is of a texture not remarkable in itself, being in colour and composition much like other salts, but hidden within its grains is a power of youth and vigour beyond the accomplishment of the most learned apothecaries. I have tasted this salt for myself (though the merchants of the place, who are extremely greedy, demand disgraceful prices for it) and I can vouch before God that its powers are real.

Six centuries later, when I crossed the Omani desert with the Sultan of Muscat and Oman in 1956, one of his slave-cooks confided in me that the Sultan would eat no salt but salt from Hav.

Thus it is that an exotic trade still binds this city to the Arab countries across the sea. The salt merchants of the Medina stand in line of the Seljuk camel-men, with their myrrh, their gold, their silks, cloves and gingers; and true successors to the dhows and feluccas of medieval Hav are the white salt ships for ever passing in and out beneath the changeless scrutiny of the Dog.

8

Very often now, as the days warm up, I rise with the trumpet, and taking my notebook, and sometimes my sketching pad, I walk down to the waterfront. I like to watch the market people, and exchange a few words with Brack, and later I often take my breakfast at one of the waterfront cafés, sitting outside and drawing pictures as I eat.

You must imagine the harbour of Hav rather like a small fiord, twisted by its central Hook so that from the quaysides of the city you cannot see the open sea, only bare sloping hillocks on each side. On the east bank, beyond New Hav, stands the isolated white villa that is the British Agency, and was once the British Residency, surrounded still by its green compound, with a tangle of radio-masts on its outbuildings and a landing-stage below. On the west bank, beyond the market and the Medina, there is nothing much but a scatter of small houses, the tower of a navigation light and a semaphore, like an old-fashioned railway signal, with black balls on a mast above. Set against the mottled jumble of the Old City and its markets, the grandiose domes of the Serai, and New Hav seedy but symmetrical on its eastern shore, the harbour of Hav looks all green, wide, cool and spacious. It reminds me sometimes of a little Sydney harbour, and sometimes of Bergen.

The historical tone of it, even now, is set by the Venetians who dominated its commerce for so long. There are two small islands in the harbour, and from my usual vantage point on the quay they look exactly like islands of the Venetian lagoon – those 'humped islands' that Shelley celebrated, running away from a far grander waterfront towards a colder sea. This is not surprising, for the buildings on them are mostly Venetian: the nearer island, still called the Lazaretto, was the Venetian quarantine station, now a jolly pleasure-garden. The further and larger one, still called Isola San Pietro, still crowned with a campanile, was leased to the Venetians as a place of confinement for prisoners-of-war and their own miscreants, and the gloomy barracks they built upon it are today Hav's only penitentiary – *'a windowless, deformed and dreary pile,/Such a one as age to age might add, for uses vile . . .'*

Then to my left, heavily arched and graced with sundry escutcheons, most of them so worn away as to be unrecognizable, stands the Fondaco di Cina, the biggest Venetian commercial building outside Venice, through which in its heyday an astonishing proportion of all the eastern trade, from Russia, from Central Asia, from the Levant, from Persia and of course from China itself was trans-shipped. In medieval times there were repeated rumours that the Venetians were about to annex Hav, as the last in their chain of islands and peninsular strongholds guarding the eastern trade routes, and looking at this building it is easy to understand why. Though it was built in Arab territory, it is an unmistakably imperial structure – just as commanding as anything the Serenissima erected in Crete, Cyprus or Corfu. It was partly a warehouse indeed, and partly a hostelry for the Venetian merchants resident in Hav, but it was also a base for the Venetian galleys based here, with slips and sheds alongside for their careening and repair. The sheds are still there, like aircraft hangars: on top of the stone pillar outside there used to stand the Lion of St Mark, bravely demonstrating his gospel upon this waterfront of Islam.

The Fondaco now is everything under the sun, as ancient waterfront buildings ought to be – in the west it would long ago have been prettied up with souvenir shops and net-hung restaurants. There are chandlers and junk shops, and alcoves stacked with crates, sacks and broken baskets, and hole-in-corner currency dealers, and financial concerns in upstairs offices whose small nameplates are hard to make out in the shadows of their passages – Cosmopolitan

Forwarding SA is one, and another is Ahmed Khalid, Hav, Dubai and Jeddah. Mr S. Assuyian announces himself as Lloyd's Agent and Representative of Lloyd Triestino. World-wide Preferential Shipping Tariffs are offered, in several languages, by a firm surprisingly named Butterworth and Sons. The great central courtyard of the Fondaco, where once the silks and spices were stored, is now an apparently insoluble shambles of trucks, wagons, cars and motorbikes, squeezing themselves in and out through the narrow street entrance at the back. And above the grand front gate on the quayside, in the apartment I suppose of the old Venetian factory governor, sits Mr Chimoun, the Captain of the Port, a masterly Lebanese.

Masterly in a kind more suggestive, even romantic, than exactly functional. Mr Chimoun seems to me to have either a less than absolute grasp of the affairs of his port, or else a most delicately selective technique – 'two blind eyes', somebody has suggested to me. But he shows a fine aesthetic appreciation of his office and its meaning. 'When I sit here at this table,' he told me the other day (not by the way some grand furnishing of the *seicento*, only an old deal desk piled with out-of-date reference books and letters of lading), 'when I sit here and look out at that splendid view – look, do you see? there is the campanile of San Pietro – when I watch our great ships sailing in' (which they all too seldom do) 'and hear the bustle of the merchants below' (he meant the hooting of trucks unable to get out of their parking place) 'and when I hear the gun go off as it has for a thousand years' (the Russians instituted the midday gun, in 1875) 'then do you know I feel myself truly to be some great signor myself – who knows? a Dandolo, a Grimaldi? You cannot think what a tremendous feeling it is, to be sitting at this table.'

At that moment the gun *did* go off, and Mr Chimoun suggested I might care to lunch with him at the café inside the courtyard, where they serve the great speciality of the Hav waterfront, urchin soup. The place was packed, every close-jammed table slurping with urchin-lovers of all ranks, from Magda the Braudelophobe, who was in a corner with two important-looking gentlemen, probably expellees from the Athenaeum, to dock-workers in their blue denims smoking between mouthfuls at long trestle tables. The soup was delectable: just as in some rare Corsican wines, perhaps one in a case of twelve, you can taste the heavenly scrub-fragrance of the *maquis*, so through the sea-urchins of this dish, the one native gastronomic miracle of Hav, every now and then there drifts a sweetish tangy sensation, more a bouquet than a taste, which is claimed to come from the gently waving sea-herbs of the northern coves.

'I much regret,' said Mr Chimoun when the waiter brought the bill, 'that the rules of my office do not permit me to entertain you to this meal, since you are not on official business. But I trust you have enjoyed it.' Not very Dandolo-like, I could not help thinking: my share was 25 dinars – 40 new pence.

But anyway the working harbour now is much more Arab then Venetian. The language one hears is chiefly Arabic, and they are mostly distinctly Arab-looking financiers, with short clipped beards and digital gold watches, who emerge from the premises of Cosmopolitan Forwarding SA. Though the fishermen are all Greeks from the off-shore island of San Spiridon, the rig of their boats, the Hav rig, is recognizably Arab of origin, and very beautiful it is – a double lateen rig, with a jib, giving the whole vessel a most gracefully slanted appearance; the boats all have engines nowadays, but they often use their sails, and when one comes into the harbour on a southern wind, canvas bulging, flag streaming, keeling gloriously with a slap-slap of waves on its prow and its bare brown-torsoed Greeks exuberantly laughing and shouting to each other, it is as though young navigators have found their way to Hav out of the bright heroic past.

The only foreign ships trading regularly into Hav are Arab – the salt ships, especially built for the trade, shallow enough to tie up at the Salt Wharf east of the Fondaco. They fly Panamanian flags actually, and were built in Norway, but they are Arab-owned, their crews are mostly Arab, and their only voyages take them back and forth, back and forth, between Hav and the Arabian Gulf. Monotonous duties, monotonous names too – *Queen of the Salt*, *King of the Salt*, *Emperor of the Salt* – but they do not look unlovely; they are low in the water, rakish, and when one of them lies alongside the wharf with its air-conditioners humming, its decks spotless and its paintwork all agleam, you might almost take it for some Arab prince's pleasure-craft (though Brack, who sailed in them for some years, seems to think the crew quarters down below rather less than sheikhly).

Out of the East too comes most of the casual sea-traffic which noses its way into the inner harbour. This is a great place still for the vagabond trade. Browning's Waring – '*What's become of Waring,/Since he gave us all the slip?*' – may have been last seen laughing in the stern-sheets of a bum-boat at Trieste, but he had his Hav period too: his real name was Alfred Domett (he eventually became Prime Minister of New Zealand) and it was here that Kinglake met him in 1834, finding him 'much as we knew him of old, only turned a chestnutty hue'. It was by sea that Hemingway first came here, arriving macho-style on a Syrian schooner but soon gravitating to the cocktails, roulette tables and steam-yachts of Casino Cove. And it was on board an Italian tramp from Alexandria that the poet C. P. Cafavy, in a rare break from the routine of his Egyptian office, sailed into Hav in 1910 to write one of the most sensual of his lyrics:

> *He did not expect me. I had wandered far*
> *since we had met in the tavern at Aleppo . . .*

Tramp steamers of a kind still come, and perhaps bring poets sometimes. They appear to bring little else anyway and seem to sail away with not much more – a few boxes of this or that, sometimes inexplicably a couple of old cars. They are mostly Syrian or Greek – sometimes Greek Cypriot, which is why we get Cypriot wines in our restaurants (the labels ripped off, just in case, and often the single word VIN substituted). Sometimes they seem to have come to Hav to die, and lie there at their moorings apparently abandoned, their decks flaking with rust, only the dimmest of lights shining, when night-time comes, from somewhere deep beneath their hatches. But they always revive unexpectedly, and when I turn up on the quay in the morning there goes the old *Malik*, or *Achelaos*, or *Thyella*, bravely puffing away, belching clouds of black smoke, down past San Pietro to the Hook and the open sea.

Coastal colliers come too, with fuel for the power station; they are unloaded at their own jetty, well down the harbour, by hundreds of labourers with sacks and baskets, and long after they sail away again a cloud of black dust is left in the air behind them. Small tankers tie up beside the oil-tanks near by, miscellaneous motorized dhows appear from nowhere in particular, and occasionally one sees those twos and threes of futuristic Japanese trawlers that seem to find their way into every corner of the Mediterranean. .

Other traffic is harder to categorize. Once when I was down on the waterfront very early indeed, before the trumpet had blown or the market had properly opened, I heard a rumble of engines up the haven, and there came stealing out of the half-light an extremely un-shipshape motor-torpedo boat, *sans* guns or torpedo tubes. It flew a faded Stars and Stripes, and when it tied up, three young men in jeans and T-shirts emerged from wheel-house and engine-room to stretch themselves upon the quay.

'Hi,' they said, as though we were at Sausalito or Martha's Vineyard.

'Hi,' said I.

'You from Chimoun?' said one.

'Certainly not. i'm just waiting for the market to warm up.'

'Oh *I'm* sorry,' he said, 'I thought maybe you were from Chimoun.'

'Is he expecting you?' I asked. They all laughed at that. 'Expecting us?' they said. 'He'd better be.'

As you see it is an irregular kind of port. They say it is inadequately dredged or even charted, which is why I have never once seen a plutocrat's yacht from the Casino enter the inlet – only Signor Biancheri's supply-launch foams confidently in and out. Mr Assuyian the Lloyd's Agent is alleged to have died years ago. It is a port of louche and easy anarchy, and its only signs of authority are Mr Chimoun behind his desk, the chequered flag above his building, and the venerable guard-ship, provided by the Italians in 1940 (it used to be their Yangtse gunboat *Arnaldo Carlotto*), which is the nearest thing to a Hav navy, but which seldom moves from its mooring at the Lazaretto.

One charming institution, nevertheless, does bring a gentle suggestion of order to this haphazard haven. It is the Electric Ferry. Looking rather like a floating London taxi, being black, all-enclosed and the same at each end, this little vehicle sets slowly and silently off promptly at seven each morning from the Fondaco on its journey across the harbour – to the market, the two islands, the New Hav promenade and then back the same way to the Fondaco, its last trip ending precisely at midnight. Its passengers are few, but its manner is inexorable. Young Chinese run it, keeping it very clean, collecting their fares in leather pouches and issuing tickets stamped in red ELECTRIC FERI HAV: and one of the most characteristic sounds of this city is the bang, bang, bang which precedes its arrival at the quay – the noise of its slatted seats being punctiliously slammed back on their hinges, to face the other way for the next voyage.

MAY

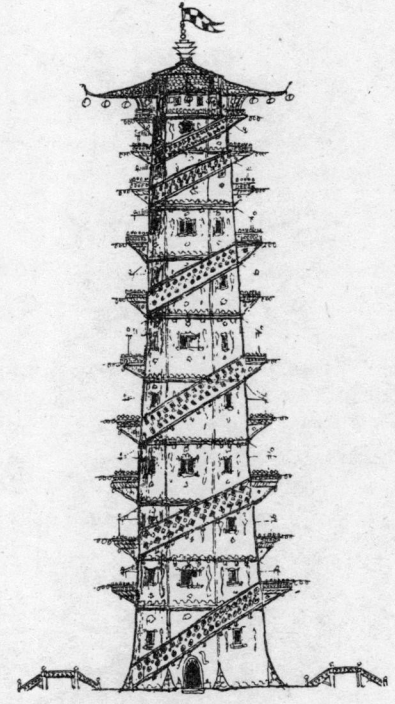

House of the Chinese Master
(after Bourdin, 1927)

9

The Roof-Race

It is 5 May, the day of the Roof-Race. As the horserace is to Siena, as the bull-running is to Pamplona, as Derby Day is to the English or even perhaps Bastille Day to the French, so the day of the Roof-Race is to the people of Hav.

It is not known for sure how this fascinating institution began, though there are plenty of plausible theories. The race was certainly being run in the sixteenth century, when Nicander Nucius described it in passing as 'a curious custom of these people'; and in 1810 Lady Hester Stanhope, the future 'Queen of Palmyra', was among the spectators: she vociferously demanded the right to take part herself, and was only dissuaded by her private physician, who said it would almost certainly be the end of her.

In later years the Russian aristocracy made a regular fête of it, people coming all the way from St Petersburg simply for the day, and lavish house-parties were organized in the villas of the western hills. Enormous stakes were wagered on the outcome; the winner, still covered with dust and sweat, was immediately taken to the Palace in the Governor's own carriage for a champagne breakfast and the presentation of the traditional golden goblet (paid for, by the way, out of an annual bequest administered by the Department of Wakfs).

Today gambling is theoretically illegal in Hav, but the goblet is still presented, more prosaically nowadays at the finishing line, and the winner remains one of the heroes of Hav for the rest of his life – several old men have been admiringly pointed out to me in the streets as Roof-Race winners of long ago. The race is so demanding that nobody over the age of twenty-five has ever run it – no woman at all yet – and only once in recorded history has it been won by the same runner twice; so that actually there is quite a community of winners still alive in Hav – the most senior extant, who owns the pleasure-garden on the Lazaretto, won the race in 1921.

The most familiar account of the race's origins is this. During a rising against the Ottoman Turks, soon after their occupation of Hav, a messenger was sent clandestinely from Cyprus to make contact with the patriotic leader Gamal Abdul Hussein, who was operating from a secret headquarters in the Medina. The messenger landed safely on the waterfront at midnight, but found every entrance to the Old City blocked, and every street patrolled by Turkish soldiers. Even as he stood there wondering how to get to Gamal, at his house behind the Grand Mosque, he was spotted by Turkish sentries and a hue and cry was raised; but far from retreating to his boat, whose crew anxiously awaited him in the darkness, without a second thought he leapt up to the ramparts of the Medina, and began running helter-skelter over the rooftops towards the mosque. Up clambered the soldiers after him, scores of them, and there began a wild chase among the chimney-pots and wind-towers; but desperately leaping over alleyways, slithering down gutters, swarming over eaves and balustrades, the messenger found his way through an upper window of Gamal's house, presented his message, and died there and then, as Hav legendary heroes must, of a cracked but indomitable heart.

Such is the popular version, the one that used to get into the guide-books – Baedeker, for instance, offered it in his *Mediterranean*, 1911, while adding that 'experienced travellers may prefer to view the tale with the usual reservations'. Magda has another version altogether, concerning the exploits of an Albanian prince, while Dr Borge regards the whole thing as pagan allegory, symbolic of summer's arrival, or possibly Christian, prefiguring the miracle of Pentecost. Most Havians, though, seem to accept the story of the messenger; and in my view, if it wasn't true in the first place, so many centuries of belief have made it true now.

The course is immensely demanding. It begins, as did the messenger's mission, with the scaling of the city wall, beside the

Market Gate, and it entails a double circuit of the entire Medina, by a different route each time, involving jumps over more than thirty alleyways, culminating in a prodigious leap over the open space in the centre of the Great Bazaar, and ending desperately in a slither down the walls of the Castle Gate to the finish. The record time for the course is just under an hour, and officials are posted all over the rooftops, beneath red umbrellas like Turkish pashas themselves, to make sure there is no cheating.

Virtually all Hav turns out for this stupendous athletic event. All shops and government offices are closed for the day, and almost the only person who cannot come to watch is Missakian the trumpeter, because it is his call from the castle rampart which is the signal for the start. In former times the race was run at midnight, as the messenger supposedly ran, but so many competitors died or were terribly injured, tripping over unseen projections, misjudging the width of lanes, that in 1882 the Russians decreed it should be run instead as dawn broke over the city – to the chagrin of those young bloods whose chief pleasure, if we are to believe Tolstoy, lay in seeing the splayed bodies falling through the street-lights to their deaths. But if it was well-ordered in Russian times, when Grand Duchesses came to watch, it is less so now: the race itself may be properly umpired and refereed, but the spectators, conveniently removed as they are from the actual course above their heads, are left absolutely uncontrolled. 'You are strong,' said Mahmoud, inviting me to join him at the great event, 'we will do the triple.'

This meant so positioning ourselves that we could see the three climactic moments of the race, one after the other – the start, the Bazaar Leap and the finish. For *aficionados* this is the *only* way to watch, and over the years dozens of ways of doing it have been devised. Some use bicycles to race around the outer circle of the walls. Some are alleged to know of passages through the city's cellars and sewers. Our system however would be simple: we would just barge our way, with several thousand others, down the clogged and excited streets from one site to the other.

Forty-two young men took part in the race this morning, and when we hastened in the half-light to join the great crowd at the Market Gate, we found them flexing their muscles, stretching themselves and touching their toes in a long line below the city wall. Two were

Chinese. One was black. One I recognized – he works at the Big Star garage, where I bought my car. One was Mahmoud's cousin Gabril, who works for the tramways company. Several wore red trunks to show that they had run the race before, in itself a mark of great distinction, and they were all heavily greased – a protection, Mahmoud said, against abrasions.

The eastern sky began to pale; the shape of the high wall revealed itself before us; from the mosque as we stood there in silence, came the call to prayer; and then from the distant castle heights sounded Missakian's trumpet. The very instant its last notes died those forty-two young men were scrabbling furiously up the stonework, finding a foothold here, a handhold there, pulling themselves up bump by bump, crack by crack, by routes which, like climbers' pitches, all have their long-familiar names and well-known characteristics. A few seconds – it cannot have been more – and they were all over the top and out of sight.

'Right,' said Mahmoud, 'quick, follow me,' and ruthlessly pushing and elbowing our way we struggled through the gate into the street that leads to the Great Bazaar in the very middle of the Medina. In sudden gusts and mighty sighs, as we progressed, we could hear spectators across the city greeting some spectacular jump, mourning some unfortunate slither – first to our right, then in front of us, then to our left, and presently behind our backs, as the runners finished their first lap. 'Quick, quick,' said Mahmoud to nobody in particular, and everyone else was saying it too – 'quick, only a few minutes now, we mustn't miss it, come along, dirleddy' – and at last we were beneath the vaulted arcade of the bazaar, lit only by shafts of sunlight through its roof-holes, shoving along its eastern axis until we found ourselves jammed with a few hundred others in the circular open space that is its apex.

We were just in time. Just as we got there we heard a wild padding of feet along the roofs above, and looking up we saw, *wham*, one flying brown body, then another, then a third, spreadeagled violently across the gap, rather like flying squirrels. One after the other they came, momentarily showed themselves in their frenzied leaps and vanished, and the crowd began to count them as they appeared – *dört, beş, altı, yedi* . . . Twenty-five came over in quick succession, then two more after a long pause, and then no more. 'Eight fallen,' said Mahmoud. 'I hope my cousin was not one' – but by then we had all begun to move off again, up the bazaar's north axis this time, to the Castle Gate. Now the crush was not so hectic. Everyone knew that the second half of the race was run much slower than the first – though the light was better by now, the terrible exertions had taken their toll. So we had time to conjecture, as we moved towards the finish line. Was that Majourian in the lead at the bazaar, or was it the formidable Cheng Lo? Who was the first Red Trunk? Had Ahmed Aziz fallen, one wondered – he was getting on a bit, after all . . . In a great sort of communal murmur we emerged from the bazaar, hurried down the Street of the Four Nomads, and passed through the Castle Gate into the square outside.

There the Governor was waiting, with the gold goblet on the table before him, attended by sundry worthies: the gendarmerie commander in his white drills and silver helmet, the chairman of the Assembly, the Catholic, Orthodox and Maronite bishops in their varied vestments, the Imam of the Grand Mosque, and many another less identifiable. There seemed to be a demonstration of some kind happening over by the Serai – a clutch of people holding banners and intermittently shouting: but the gendarmes were keeping them well away, and the dignitaries were not distracted. They did not have long to wait, anyway. Those spurts of wonder and commiseration grew closer and closer. The Governor joked benignly, as governors will, to ever-appreciative aides. The churchmen chatted ecumenically. The gendarmerie commander resolutely turned his back on the scuffles by the Serai. Splosh! like a loose sack of potatoes the first of the roof-runners, without more ado, suddenly fell, rather than jumped or even scrambled, down the sheer face of the gateway, to lie heaving, greased, bruised and bloody at the Governor's feet. Every few seconds then the others arrived, those that were still in the race. They simply let themselves drop from the gate-tower, plomp, like stunt-men playing corpses in western movies, to lie there at the bottom in crumpled heaps, or flat on their backs in absolute exhaustion.

It looked like a battlefield. The crowd cheered each new deposit, the dignitaries affably clapped. And when the winner had sufficiently recovered to receive his prize, the Governor, taking good care, I noticed, that none of the grease, blood or dust got on his suit, kissed him on both cheeks to rapturous cries of 'Bravo! Bravo the Victor!' rather as though we were all at the opera.

'Who won?' demanded Missakian, looking up from his beans and newspaper as we entered the station café for our breakfast. 'Izmic,' said Mahmoud. 'Izmic!' cried Missakian disgustedly, and picking up his trumpet he blew through it a rude unmusical noise.

10

*To Little Yalta – 'fresh start' – Russian Hav – Diaghilev and Nijinsky –
the graveyard*

Boulevard de Cetinje, which slices its way so arrogantly through
the Medina, turns into something nicer when it crosses the canal and
winds into the western hills. Though it is little more than a rutted
track now, you can see that it was once an agreeable country avenue.
Many of its trees are dead and gone, but the survivors are fine old
Hav catalpas, sometimes so rich, if decrepit, that they lean right
across the road and touch each other. Halfway to the sea, at a crest
of the road, there is a little wooden pavilion, showing traces of blue
paint upon it; at weekends a girl sells fruit, biscuits and lemonade
there, to lugubrious Havian music from her transistor, and outside
there are pretty little rustic tables and benches, and the remains of a
flower-garden.

This is the road the Russians built, purely for their own convenience, in the days of Imperial Hav. Many a memoir mentions the
little blue pleasure-pavilion on the road to the sea. And when, like
the princes and Grand Duchesses; the generals and the courtesans of
long ago, you emerge from the hills a few miles further on, there
before you, on a wide sandy bay beside the glistening sea, stand the
houses of the small bathing resort they used to call Malaya Yalta,
Little Yalta. They are hardly houses really, only glorified bathing
huts, to which the servants would hurry beforehand with food and
wine, to get the samovars going and put out the parasols, but from
a distance they look entertainingly imposing. Each with its own
wooded stockade, they are merrily embellished with domes, turrets,

spires, ornate barge-boarded verandahs and ornamental chimney-pots. It looks like a goblin Trouville down there, full of colour and vivacity: it is only when the road peters out at the remains of the boardwalk that you find it all to be a spectral colony, its fences collapsed, its verandahs sagging, its paintwork flaked away, its comical little towers precariously listing, and only three or four of its once-festive houses at the northern end remaining, occupied by sad families of Indian squatters.

Even the ghosts of those who were happy here have left the seashore now.

There are a very few old Russians, still alive in Hav, who can just remember the bright pleasures of Little Yalta. The most prominant of them is Anna Novochka, who lives alone with a housekeeper in the very last of the old patrician villas of the western hills still to be inhabited. She is a dauntless old lady. Though she is now in her nineties, and almost penniless, she dresses always in bright flowing colours, blouses of swathed silk, brocade skirts which I suspect to have been made out of curtain fabric. 'We Russians,' she likes to say, 'are people of colour. We *need* colour, as other people need liberty.'

I often go to see her, to take tea in her sparse and airy drawing-room (where pale squares upon the walls show where pictures used to hang), followed often enough, as we talk into the evening, by glasses of vodka with squeezed lime juice. She was not always called Novochka. Like many of the Russians who stayed in Hav after the Revolution, she adopted a new name of her own invention: she says it means 'Fresh Start'. Her housekeeper is Russian too, but of more recent vintage; she came to Hav via Israel five or six years ago, and is, so Anna tells me, totally disenchanted with everything. She does look rather sour. Anna herself on the other hand is the very incarnation of high spirits, and in her I feel I am meeting the miraculously preserved mood of Imperial Hav itself.

For Russian Hav was nothing if not high-spirited. It was, of course, very artificial and snobbish, like all such colonies – 'Why must you always be talking of Hav?' says Chekov's Vasilyev to his friend Gregory (in *An Affair*). 'Isn't our town good enough for you then? In Hav you never hear a word of Russian, I'm told, nothing but French and German is good enough down there.' But it seems to have possessed a certain underlying innocence. The Russians eagerly accepted Hav, under the Pendeh Agreement of 1875, as their only outlet to the Mediterranean (having lost the Ionian Islands to the British half a century before), and as a stepping-stone perhaps towards those Holy Places of Jerusalem which meant so much to them in those days. They knew well enough, though, that strategically it was useless to them – its harbour hopelessly shallow, its position fearfully vulnerable. To these disadvantages they cheerfully reconciled themselves, and instead set out to make the place as thoroughly agreeable as they could.

Politically, of course, it was an absolute despotism – Hav had never been anything else – but the Russian yoke was light enough, minorities were not suppressed, opinions were given reasonable latitude. At the end of the nineteenth century indeed Hav became a favourite destination for young Russian revolutionaries on the run, until in 1908 somebody blew up the Governor's private railway coach, and Count Kolchok was obliged to accept a detachment of the secret police.

Even the grandiose buildings around Pendeh Square – more grandiose still before the Cathedral of the Annunciation and the Little Pushkin Theatre were burnt down in the 1920s – even those somewhat monstrous buildings are generally agreed to be fun. They may have been intended to blazon Russia's Mediterranean presence to the world, but at least they did so exuberantly. Anna says that in her girlhood, before the First World War, they used to be positively dazzling in their golds and blues, their gardens exquisitely maintained and the gravel of the avenue in front of the Palace raked and smoothed so constantly that it looked like 'coral sand, when the tide has just gone out'. And the villas in the hills, where most of the richer Russians preferred to live, seem, if Anna's memories are true, to have been the happiest places imaginable.

'You must realize there are so few of us. We were all friends – enemies too of course, but friends at the same time. Many of us were related. I had three cousins living in Hav at one time. Kolchok himself was a relative on my mother's side. And when *le haut monde* came down for the season from Moscow and St Petersburg, why, we knew all of them too – or if we didn't, we very soon did. It was like the very nicest of clubs. And everyone felt freer here, far from the

Court, without estates to worry about, or serfs I suppose in the old days. We were Russia emancipated!'

In the high summer season Hav was terrifically festive. To and fro between the villas went the barouches and the horsemen, laughing in the evening. Trundling hilariously down the road to the sea went the bathing parties, stopping at the blue pavilion to clamour for lemonades. Ever and again the waltzes rang out from the garden of the Palace, and the coaches and cars jammed the great square outside, and the lights shone, and long after midnight one heard the footmen calling for carriages – 'No. 23, His Imperial Highness the Grand Duke Felix . . . No. 87, the Countess Kondakov!' Little sailing boats with canopies used to take the ladies and children for decorous trips around the harbour, to the Lazaretto pleasure-gardens, down to the Iron Dog, while the young men sometimes rented dhows to sail around the southern point and meet their families at Malaya Yalta.

'Were you never bored, with so much unremitting pleasure?'

'Never. But then I was only a little girl, remember. I see it all through the eyes of childhood. Never have I been so excited, never in all my life, as I used to be when we were taken to the station to see the first train of the season arrive. It was a fixed day, you know, announced beforehand in the *Court Gazette* and so on, and the first train was one of the great events of the year. We were allowed to stay up especially! We would all wear our best clothes, and all the barouches and luggage-traps would be waiting out there in the square – oh, I remember it so clearly! – and it used to seem like *hours* till the train arrived. We could hear it hooting, hooting, all the way through the Balad.

'And then, when it came at last, the excitement! All the grand ladies in the latest fashions, fashions we'd never seen before, and the gentlemen in their tall hats, with carnation buttonholes, and Kolchok would be there to greet whatever princess or Grand Duke was on board, and then he'd go around welcoming old friends and kissing cousins and so forth, and everybody else would be embracing their friends and laughing, and we children would be hopping up and down with the fun of it. And then all the servants jumping off from the coaches behind, and the bustle and fuss of getting the luggage together, and out we'd clop from Pendeh Square like a kind of army. It was so colourful, you have no idea. When we got home, before we children were packed off to bed, we were allowed to have a cup of cocoa with the grown-ups.

'My father said to me once, "Whatever you forget in life, don't forget the pleasure of this evening with our friends." I never have, as you see. I can hear him saying it now! And now all those friends are gone, only one old woman living on and remembering them.'

Between 1910 and 1914 the supreme event of the Hav social calendar was the annual visit of the Diaghilev Ballet to the Little Pushkin Theatre. Diaghilev first came to Hav in 1908, was fascinated by the place, and was easily persuaded to bring his company from Paris for a week at the height of the season each year. Diaghilev in Hav became, for those few brief summers, one of the great festivities of Czarist Russia, and hundreds of people used to come by special train for the performances.

A huge marquee was erected in Pendeh Square for the week, and there after each night's performance dancers and audience alike dined, drank champagne, danced again and ate urchins into the small hours, in a magical aura of fairy lights and music, beneath the velvet skies of Hav. In 1910 the French novelist Pierre Loti, then a naval officer, was in Hav for one night during the first Diaghilev season, his ship having anchored off-shore. 'It was like a dream to me,' he wrote afterwards, 'to come from my ship into this midnight celebration. The music of the orchestra floated about the square and rebounded, I thought, from the golden domes of the Palace. The ladies floated in and out of the great tent like fairies of the night – white arms, billowing silk skirts, shining diamonds. The men were magnificent in black, with their bright sashes and glittering orders, Diaghilev himself occupying the centre of the stage. And in and amongst this elegant throng there flitted and pranced the dancers of the ballet, still in their costumes – fantastic figures of gold and crimson, moving through the crowd in movements that seemed to me hardly human. When I walked across the square to the picket-boat awaiting me at the quay I saw a solitary figure like a feathered satyr dancing all alone with wild movements up the long avenue of palms outside the Palace. It was Nijinsky.'

It was said of Nijinsky that he was never happier than he was in Hav, and he is remembered still with proud affection. 'I saw Nijinsky clear' is a leitmotif of elderly reminiscence in Hav, among Arabs and Turks as often as among the Europeans of the concessions. He used to love to wander the city by himself, an image so unforgettable that old people describe him as though they can actually see him still. Sometimes he would be on the harbour-front, watching the ships. Sometimes the trumpeter, arriving at Katourian's bastion, would find the great dancer already there. He liked to go to the station to see the train leave in the morning. And Anna one day, hunting among her souvenirs in a black leather box full of papers, pictures, twists of hair, postage stamps, imperial securities – 'Securities! Some securities!' – produced for me a photograph of Nijinsky taken on an outing, it said in spindly French on the back, in 1912.

There were only two figures in the picture, against a background of sky and bare heathland. One was the Iron Dog, full face. Beside it, ramrod stiff, wearing a kind of peasant jerkin and baggy trousers, Nijinsky stared expressionless into the lens, his hair ruffled by the wind.

The Ballet Russe, they say, was deeply influenced by its association with Hav. Bakst the great designer was seduced by the peculiar colour combinations he found here – the Russian dazzle of golds, crimsons and bright blues set against skies, seas and heathy hills that expressed a different sensibility. Benois was so taken with the Hav costume – straw hat and *gallabiyeh* – that he introduced it into the fair scenes of *Petrushka*. Diaghilev himself seems to have been calmed and comforted by the city's blend of the heady and the sombre, the exhilarated and the brooding; he is buried in Venice, but Anna says she herself heard him say that he would like to lie in the little Russian graveyard overlooking the sea in the western hills of Hav.

The graveyard is forlornly neglected now, though its windbreak of dark cypresses makes it visible from far away, like a war cemetery. It lies on a slope of the hill, looking out over the western bay and Pyramid Rock; from its lower graves you can just see the faded baubles of Little Yalta. Dominating the plot is the tall obelisk that marks Count Kolchok's grave, with a portrait in bas-relief and a long Russian epitaph. There are a few lesser obelisks, and a couple of broken columns, and some mourning angels. Mostly, though, they are simple crosses, some of wood, that mark the last resting places of

Hav's Russians. Often their inscriptions have long been obliterated, by the heat, and the winds off the sea; everywhere the coarse grass grows, and here and there the scrub off the heath has broken through the surrounding wall. Soon it will have obliterated all but those obelisks, and an elevated angel or two.

11

A quality of fantasy – around the great square – House of the Chinese Master – New Hav – a bit of a lark – the Conveyor Bridge

When Marco Polo came to Hav in the thirteenth century, he was struck not so much by the wealth or power of the city, but by something unusual to its nature. 'This is a place of strange buildings and rites, not like other places.' Modern Hav is not perhaps exactly beautiful – it is too knocked about for that, has been infiltrated by too many shabby purlieus, frayed by too many reverses of fortune. But it does still possess some quality of fantasy, something almost frivolous despite its ancient purposes, and this is caused I think by its particular criss-cross mixture of architectural styles, which makes many of its buildings feel like exhibition structures, or aesthetic experiments. Add to this piquancy of melange a certain flimsiness of construction – Hav bricks are small and slight, Hav roofs look lightly laid upon their joists – and the impression is given of a monumental but neglected folly, built by a sequence of playful potentates for their own amusement down the centuries.

The one Hav prospect that occasionally gets into picture-books, having been painted by numberless artists of the T. Ramotsky school, is the view looking northward from the waterfront towards the castle. Deposited here without warning out of the blue, you really might be at a loss to know where on this earth you were. To the right stands the hulk of the Fondaco, built of red brick brought from Venice, with its four squat corner towers, its machicolations, and its arcading half-filled now with hoardings and concrete walls. In the background, splendidly blocking the scene, the hill of the acropolis is crowned with the ruin of the castle, Beynac's keep mouldering at the summit, Saladin's gateway good as new below. To the left rise the walls of the Medina, protruded over by wind-towers, minarets and the upper floors of the huge merchant houses beside the bazaars.

And in the centre, seen across the busy traffic of the quay, is the official complex created by the Russians to celebrate their presence on this southern shore. The square itself, with its equestrian emperor in the centre, is said to be bigger than the Grand Square at Isfahan upon whose proportions the Arabs originally based it, and is bounded left and right by double lines of palm trees; between the eastern avenue the tramline runs, between the western is the gravel footpath along which Loti saw Nijinsky dance, originally preserved for Russian officials and their ladies, now a favourite public dalliance. The waterfront end of the square is marked by a line of bollards, placed there by the Venetians and made from captured Genoese guns; at the other end, where the winding path to the castle starts, there is a handsome double terrace, with urns and lions couchant on it, and in the middle a big circular fountain which, for all its dolphins, nymphs and bearded sea-gods, alas no longer founts.

Then to the east and west, more like pavilions than substantial buildings, rise the showy display pieces of Russian Hav, Serai on one side, station on the other. Their symbolism is extravagant, and entertaining. They represent Mediterranean Russia – the achievement at last of a dream as much aesthetic, or imaginative, as political. High above them tower the gilded onion domes, capped with gay devices, which instantly summon in the mind bitter steppes and snowy cities of the north – something of the sleigh and the fur hat, the samovar and perhaps the OGPU too – Mother Russia, at once smilingly and authoritatively embodied, here at the end of the railway line.

But below these bright globules, which somehow manage to be a little grim, as well as flashy, the architects Schröter and Huhn (who also designed the gigantic garrison cathedral at Tiflis, up the line) built in a very different allegory: for the tall arches and arcades below the domes, the gardens surrounding them, the inner courtyards and the long interior corridors are built in what architects Schröter and Huhn conceived as Southern Eclectic. Ogive arches in multi-coloured brick sustain that Slavic roofline, and there are high balconies with hoods, as in great houses of Syria, and even *mashrabiya* windows here and there. The courtyards are Alhambran, with prim patterns of orange trees; the tall shuttered windows of the wings might be in Amalfi or the old part of Nice.

Seen in the general rather than the particular, against the high silhouette of the castle hill, this ensemble really is rather spectacular, a little muted though its colours are now, a little skew-whiff some of its shutters and rickety the less frequented of its balconies: and especially seen from the Electric Ferry, sliding quietly across the harbour, all those strange and disparate shapes, the towered severity of the Fondaco, the bright domes, the stark castle walls above, seem as they shift one against the other oddly temporary, as though one of these days the Grand Hav Exhibition must come to an end, and all its pavilions be dismantled.

The most celebrated architectural hybrid of Hav is the House of the Chinese Master in the Medina, directly outside the west entrance of the Great Bazaar. In the Middle Ages, when the Venetians were paramount upon the waterfront of Hav, the Chinese established a financial ascendancy in the city, and in 1432 the Amir was obliged to allow them a merchant headquarters actually within the Medina walls – hitherto they had been confined to their own settlement of Yuan Wen Kuo. They built it essentially in the glorious Ming style of the age, to plans said to have been sent from Beijing by the architect of the Qian Qing Gong, the Palace of Heavenly Purity in the Forbidden City; but they were subtle enough to make of it something specific to Hav. It is the westernmost of all the major buildings of Chinese architecture, and some say the finest Chinese construction west of the Gobi: discovering it for the first time out of the darkness of the Great Bazaar is perhaps the most astonishing aesthetic experience Hav can offer.

Imagine yourself jostling a way through those souks, shadowy, dusty, clamorous, argumentative, and approaching gradually, past charm-hawker and water-seller, blaring record shop and clatter of iron-smiths, the small yellow rectangle of sunshine that marks the end of the arcade. So great is the contrast of light that at first there is nothing to be distinguished but the dazzle itself; but as you get closer, and your eyes accustom themselves to the shine, you see resolving itself out there what seems to be a gigantic piece of black fretwork – multitudinous squares, triangles, circles and intersections, with daylight showing intricately through them. Is it some kind of huge screen? Is it something to do with the mosque, or an antique defence work? No: when you reach the end of the corridor at last, and step outside into the afternoon, you realize with delight that you have reached Qai Chen Bo, the House of the Chinese Master.

It *is* a house, and a very large one, but its inner chambers and offices, long since converted into a warren of tenements, are surrounded by a nine-sided mesh of elaborately worked black marble, forming in fact an endlessly spiralling sequence of balconies, but looking from the outside wonderfully lacy and insubstantial. The building is eleven storeys high, deliberately built a storey higher, so legend says, than any of the Arab structures of the city, and it is capped by a conical roof of green glazed tiles, heavily eaved and surrounded by pendant bobbles. It is reached by five wooden bridges over a nine-sided moat, once filled with fish and water-lilies, now only with rubbish: at each angle of the moat a separate small circular pool festers. The building is hemmed in nowadays by nondescript brick and concrete blocks, but still stands there sublimely individual and entertaining – after five hundred years and more, much the liveliest building in Hav.

In 1927 Professor Jean-Claude Bourdin of the Académie française wrote a pamphlet about this building. All sorts of allusions, it seems, can be read into a construction that looks to the innocent eye no more than a splendid *jeu d'esprit*. The fundamental shape of the building is, of course, that of the pagoda, the most unmistakably Chinese of forms, with its wide eaves and its gently tapering flanks – the Arabs were to be left in no doubt, not for a moment, as to the nationality of the Master. In the five bridges there is apparently a direct reference to the five bridges over the Golden Water River in the Forbidden City, an allusion that would imply to the Chinese themselves, if hardly to anyone else, the presence here of the imperial authority. Then the moat itself, with its nine unblinking eye-pools, is claimed by Professor Bourdin to be a figure of the Lake of Sleepless Diligence, while the high corridor which bisects the ground floor of the building, west to east, is said to be exactly aligned upon Tian

Tan, the Temple of the Heavens in Beijing. Finally, so Bourdin thinks, the whole edifice, so complex and deceptive, is a sophisticated architectural metaphor of the maze.

Well I'm sure he was right – he was a corresponding member of the Chinese Academy, too – but for me the House of the Chinese Master, whatever its subliminal purposes, is above all the most cheerful of follies. It is a building that makes nearly everyone, seeing it for the first time, laugh with pleasure, so droll is its posture there, so enchantingly delicate its construction, and so altogether unexpected its presence among the severities of medieval Islam. Here is what other visitors have written of it:

Pero Tafur, 1439: 'I have seen no building like this masterpiece, not in Rome, Venice or in Constantinople, and indeed I think it is the most remarkable and delightful of all buildings.'

Nicandur Nucius, 1546: 'The House of the Chinese Master at Hav is the merry wonder of all who see it.'

Anthony Jenkinson, 1558: 'In that part of the city where the Amir lives is a tall tower built by the Chinamen, exceeding ingenious and merry, so that had it not been for the severe scrutiny of the Mussulmans close by we would fain have burst out laughing at the spectacle.'

Alexander Kinglake, 1834: 'Do you remember when we were boys together we would make houses in the trees for our childish entertainments? Well, you must imagine all the tree-houses that ever were constructed pushed all on top of one another, and crowned with the wide straw hat that our good Mrs W used to wear to church on Sundays.'

Mark Twain, 1872: 'If I hadn't seen it with my own eyes I would have said it was more probably the House of the Chinese Teller of Tales – but there it was before me, and I could not have told a taller tale myself.'

D. H. Lawrence, 1922: 'A hideous thing. Restless, unsatisfied. And yet one could not help smiling at the vivid, brisk and out-flinging insolence of it.'

Robert Byron, 1927: 'Surrounded by the sombre piles of Islam, the House of the Chinese Master burst into our view in a flowering of spectacular eccentricity. It was impossible to leave the city after so brief a glimpse of this prodigy; sighing, we resolved to come back in the morning. "You don't want to see inside now?" nagged the wretched guide. "Alas, it is not allowed," said David at once. "We are Rosicrucians." '

But I will leave the last comment to Sigmund Freud, who lived for a time in modest lodgings on the eighth floor of the house: 'It is difficult for me to express how profound an effect this experience has had upon me. It is as though I have lived within the inmost cavity of a man's mind – and that the mind of a Chinese architect dead for five hundred years. No number of hours spent in analysis with my patients has brought me nearer to the sources of personality than the weeks I spent, all unthinking, in the House of the Chinese Master.'

I suppose you could say the very notion of New Hav is cross-bred – critics certainly thought so when it was founded, and historians sometimes say so now. It was certainly a quixotic gesture, to choose this remote and inessential seaport for so advanced an experiment in internationalism. As to the construction of a brand-new city to house the concessionary areas, that was variously considered at the time as either an act of preposterous extravagance, or else a project nobly worthy of the age that was dawning after the war to end all wars.

An international committee of architects was invited to design New Hav, and the plan they drew up was patently consensus architecture, a little dull. What it lacks in genius, however, it makes up for in an unexpected and sometimes comic caprice of detail. The idea was to balance the roughly circular walled city of the Arabs, on the western side of the harbour, with a second walled city on the eastern side, leaving the Serai and the castle in between. The harbour gate of New Hav, opening on to a promenade upon the western quay, looks directly across the harbour to the Market Gate of the Medina. At the same time, the northern axis of the new city was to be aligned upon the castle hill, so that you could see the rock of the acropolis from the very middle of New Hav; but since this did not in the event prove possible in the city's geometrically tripartite form, the northern boulevard had to be twisted out of true, causing agonizing disputes between the French and the Italians, whose concessions it separated (in the end the Italians were compensated by being given possession of the promenade upon the harbour).

Everything else about New Hav is excessively symmetrical, and there is almost nothing that is not balanced by something else, and almost no vista that is not suitably closed. From the central Place des Nations, below my balcony, radiate the three dividing boulevards, Avenue de France northwards towards the Serai and the castle hill, Viale Roma westwards to the harbour, Unter den Südlinden eastwards towards nowhere in particular. The city was supposed to be a physical representation of the League's visionary initiative – a place of reconciliation and cooperation, of unity in variety. Its circular shape was meant to symbolize eternal peace, and each boulevard was planted with a different species of tree (planes, catalpas and ilexes) to express the joy of amicable difference.

The façades of Place and boulevards are all uniform – grandly neo-classical, in a Beaux-Arts style, arcaded at street level, mansard-roofed above – and they are marked with elegant tiled street signs, in four languages, contributed to this old haven of the Armenians by the Armenian Pottery in Jerusalem. But the liberty allowed to the powers to do what they like in their own quarters saves the place from sterile monumentality. Resolutely internationalist though they were, none of the three could resist the claims of patriotism when they were let loose on the side-streets, and there are few facets of French, Italian or German architecture that are not represented somewhere within the pattern of New Hav. There are mock-Bavarian inns. There is a music-hall (the Lux Palace) straight from Montmartre. There is a classic Fascist railway station, modelled on Milan's, which since no railway enters New Hav, was used as the Italian Post Office instead. If the French decided to build a cathedral, what else but a little Rheims would do? If the Germans wanted a Residenz, what but a small *Schloss*? Though everything is cracked and peeling now, it is all there to this day, Beaux-Arts to Bauhaus, neo-Imperial to late Nihilist (the Casa Frioli in the Italian quarter, a marvel of swirled concrete decorated with mosaics of glaring purple, is the least avoidable building in New Hav).

Two world-famous architects are represented. The glass-and-

concrete Maison de la Culture in the French quarter, with its stilts
and green cladding, is one of Le Corbusier's less inspired works: in
it, between the wars, everyone from Colette to Malraux gave lectures
on The Meaning of Frenchness or Allegory in Provençal Folk-Dance.
More importantly, you may notice scattered fitfully through the
German quarter a certain distinction of design in matters electrical:
lamp-standards, light-switches, even a few antique electric fires and
toasters all seem to obey some central directive of taste. This is
because the German administration entrusted the power system of
its quarter to the Berlin company AEG, and it was their great
consultant architect Peter Behrens who, during a visit to Hav in
1925, drew up designs for the whole electrical network. Unfortu-
nately he had no say in the power station, which had been built by
the Russians and supplied the whole peninsula, but within the
German quarter everything electrical was his – the bold transformer
station, like a whale-back beside the Ostgatte, the powerful street-
light pylons, the solid square switches of brown bakelite. Of course
much of it is lost, but even now, so ubiquitous was Behren's
influence, there is a kind of subliminal strength to the style of the
German quarter which is distributed, I like to think, directly through
the frequently fused and multitudinously patched circuits of AEG-
Hav.

For the rest, there is nothing of supreme quality. It is all a bit of
a lark. All was done, one feels, even the Italian Post Office, in a spirit
of genial optimism, elevated sometimes into parody. Architectural
purists of the 1920s sneered mercilessly at New Hav, and Lutyens,
invited to attend its formal opening in 1928, said privately that it
reminded him of the ghost train on Brighton pier, so dizzy did it
make him, and so often did damp objects slap him in the face.

But at least it possesses, as few such artificial towns do, an air of
hopeful guilelessness. Just this once, it seems to say, just for this
moment, even our separate patriotisms are merely amusing. And
most guilelessly amusing of all, to my mind, are the three arches by
which each radial boulevard, as it debouches into the central Place,
is ornamentally bridged. I can see all three from my terrace, if I lean
out far enough. Close to the left a replica of the Bridge of Sighs
ambiguously links our quarter with the French. Further round the
Place, the Avenue de France is spanned by a squashed and potted

representation of the towered bridge at Cahors. And opposite me stands an elevated Brandenburg Gate, splendid indeed when a No. 2 tram comes storming underneath with its rocking red trailer.

Armand thinks them all very silly, but he should not scorn Hav's follies, for the most gloriously ludicrous of them all was contributed by his own country. In those days it was an official French custom to distribute among Francophone communities across the world small iron replicas of the Eiffel Tower, still to be seen in places like Mauritius or Madagascar. It was thought improper, I suppose, to make such an offering to Tripartite Hav, so instead the French government presented the Conveyor Bridge which spans the harbour mouth beside the Iron Dog, perhaps ten miles south of the city centre, as a gesture of France's profound respect for the people and civilization of the peninsula. Only the French could build conveyor bridges – archetype was Lanvedin's magnificent Pont Transbordent at Marseilles – so its unmistakable outline on the finest site in Hav would be a perpetual reminder of French skill and generosity.

No matter that almost nobody wanted to cross the harbour down there, or that the elaborate solution of a conveyor bridge was perfectly unnecessary anyway. The French mind was majestically made up, and to this day the bridge operates with the help of generous subsidies from Paris – besides being, thanks to its regular mainten- ance by French engineers, the most efficient piece of mechanism in Hav. Twelve times a day its platform, slung on steel wires from the girders high above, sets off in a gentle swaying motion across the harbour mouth, guided by a captain wearing a derivation of French naval uniform in his small wooden cabin in the middle. The pace is measured. The machinery is silent. A long chequered pennant streams from the cabin roof. To the north you can see the castle, rising on its rock above the city, to the south the Mediterranean sea lies blue, green and flecked with foam. Below you, perhaps, a white salt ship slips elegantly out of the haven for Port Said and the Red Sea. In all Hav there is nothing much more foolish than the Conveyor Bridge – but nothing much grander, either!

12

The Iron Dog – graffiti – on Greeks – on Greekness – something haunting

Last week, for the first time, I stood like Nijinsky beside the Iron Dog.

You can reach it direct from the Medina, but I preferred to approach the beast from the east, snout-on so to speak; so I drove through the German gate of New Hav after breakfast, took the rough track around the back of the British Agency, and arrived at the Conveyor Bridge in time for the nine o'clock crossing (which for myself I think of as a flight, so airy is the motion of that platform beneath its spindly wires, with its wind-indicator swirling and its pennant streaming bravely). The other passengers were all Greeks – a man in a truck, three black-shawled women with an empty pony cart. As we approached the western shore, I noticed, the eyes of us all, even the captain's, were drawn to the enigmatic creature on its high headland; and when we drew level with it, almost at the same height as our platform, all the women crossed themselves.

For the bridge disgorges its passengers a little way inland from the Dog, and you must walk back along the windswept moor to get to it. No good taking the car, for there is no track, and the ground is thick with scented scrub – so scented that it fills the air with its fragrance, and is said to give an intoxicating bouquet to the water from the spring which, sprouting halfway up the sea-cliff, is thought to be the reason why the Greeks landed here in the first place. The wind blew about me, then, the captain waved from his high gazebo, and through the perfumed sunshine I walked towards the most celebrated of all Hav's monuments.

It was not, when I reached it, how I had foreseen. From a distance it looks all stark arrogance, its head held so high, its tail outstretched, its legs, slightly splayed, planted fiercely in the ground. It has been called the Iron Dog at least since the eleventh century, when the Crusaders wrote the earliest descriptions we possess; but so relentless does it appear, especially in photographs, that some modern scholars have declared it to be not a dog at all, but rather the fox that young Spartans were supposed to take into the hills, to gnaw at their bellies and make men of them. 'I can never see a picture of that animal,' wrote T. E. Lawrence, who subscribed to the theory himself, 'without feeling a pain in my tum.'

But when you get close to the figure, such notions seem implausible. Whatever else he may be, the Iron Dog is certainly not a fox. His face is genial. His legs are implanted not ferociously at all, but playfully. His elongated tail streams eagerly, as though he is only waiting the word to spring after grouse or gazelle. He is made of bronze, with the remains of gilt showing on it, but so subtly is he structured, and so infinite are the little cracks of time and weather that layer his skin, that the material looks more like wood, and makes the figure seem remarkably light – especially as its big metal plinth has long since disappeared into the soil, turf and scrub.

The Iron Dog is about six feet high, paw to ear, and there are many graffiti on his hide. There is the famous rune, companion to that on one of the Arsenal lions in Venice, which proclaims that men of the Byzantine emperor's Norse bodyguard once landed on this peninsula. There are indecipherable scratches in Greek. A very hazy M.P., on the animal's rear flank, is popularly supposed to be Marco Polo's. There are some marvellously flowery little ciphers which have been identified as the marks of Venetian silk merchants, and scores of stranger devices, apparently of all ages, which seem to have some cabalistic meaning. Henry Stanley the explorer, who came here after the opening of the Suez Canal in 1869, has signed himself shamelessly beneath the animal's chin. More disgracefully still a large crowned eagle, deeply and professionally chiselled, commemorates the visit here of Kaiser Wilhelm, on his way to Jerusalem.

Disgraceful, and yet . . . There is something intensely moving about those mementoes, cut, all down the centuries, in the skin of so ancient a beast. I found a stone and added my own emblem (I will not tell you what), establishing my line of succession, too, to the first of all the peoples who have put ashore in Hav. Here as everywhere, one likes to lay claim to the heritage of the Greeks.

The modern Greeks of Hav certainly enjoy it. If I have been told once, I have been told a thousand times about the lost glories of the Hav acropolis, about Schliemann and Achilles, about the great Spartan assault, in the fourth century BC, whose siege-work was the still recognizable canal, and whose triumphant trophy is supposedly the Iron Dog. 'Hav is essentially a Greek city,' said the Orthodox bishop boldly when I went to see him in his palace beside the cathedral. 'It is the last of the Greek colonies along the shore of Asia Minor.' But then he is profoundly prejudiced against everything Turkish, including Turkish geography. He frequently calls the Turkish people barbarians, and once publicly declared them to be the enemies of God. I asked him if this was not playing with fire, Hav being where and what it was. He merely shrugged his brawny shoulders. 'I think what I think, I say what I say.'

Others of the Greek community are more cautious. The Greek shops and loan offices which have always proliferated in the Balad rarely announce themselves in Greek script nowadays, and many of their owners, I am told, have adopted Turkish or Arabic names. Several people important in the administration are supposed to have concealed Greek origins.

'Do you really suppose your friend Mahmoud is an Arab? Some Arab! He's no more Arab than Missakian's Armenian!'

'Missakian's not Armenian?'

'Of course not. He's pure Greek, anyone can see that, like half the people in this place who call themselves Armenian, or Jewish, or Syrian . . .'

'Dear God,' I said to Magda one day, trying to assimilate all these confusions, 'I don't think I shall ever master the meaning of Hav.' 'The meaning of Hav is easy,' she said coldly, 'it's the meaning of Greeks that's hard.'

Certainly theirs is a somewhat shadowy presence in the city. There seem to be no Greeks at the Athenaeum. I have noticed none in the bar of the Adler-Hav, or listening to the jazz at the Bristol, and there were certainly no Greek names on the roster of the roof-runners. Signora Vattani scoffs when I remark upon these facts. 'Of course there are no Greeks in *society*. Greeks are shopkeepers. You never saw a Greek in New Hav, in the old days, unless he was delivering the groceries. If you want to meet Greeks, you must go to the Balad.' But the bishop gave me different advice. 'To see the Hav Greek as he really is – to see the true Havian, in fact – you should visit St Spiridon. You have seen the Iron Dog. Now go and see the people who created it.' He himself was born on the island, and he gave me, there and then, a letter of introduction to his sister Kallonia – 'It means beautiful in our dialect,' he said, 'but I'm sorry to say she isn't.'

A ferry goes there once a day, out in the morning, back in the afternoon, so yesterday I drove to the ferry station, which is near the south-eastern extremity of peninsular Hav, and joined the islanders for the crossing. The little steamboat was packed to its gunwales – women in black sitting on piles of their own parcels, powerful men with moustaches smoking bitter pipes, young bloods with motorbikes singing to the music of their transistors, children scampering everywhere, mules, horses, brawny dogs with spiked collars, the inescapable priest in his tall black hat and a few cheerful girls in cotton frocks.

The crossing takes half an hour – the ferry-boat is elderly, the currents there, sweeping in and out of China Bay, are very strong – and by the time we had tied up at the island dock, I swear, nobody on that ship was unaware of my purposes. I could almost hear the intelligence running around those decks: 'She's a writer – Iron Dog – Greeks – Kallonia Laskaris – saw the Bishop – Kallonia – writer – Iron Dog . . .' And when we disembarked, amid a little harbour settlement of tin shacks that looked more like western Canada than eastern Mediterranean, three or four of the women, and an indeterminate number of dogs and children, guided me up the hill through the celery fields to the Laskaris house, which seemed to occupy the very centre and apex of the island.

Well, it was true, Kallonia was not very beautiful, but she was extremely kind, and in no time at all she had fixed up a lunch for me – 'just to meet a few of our people, you must get the *truth* about us in your writing'. But first she detailed her daughter Arianna, eleven years old to show me round the island. This was not difficult. It is only about a mile round, and is speckled all over, as by pimples, with small stone houses like Kallonia's own, each with its pergola and its garden. The only village is the little ferry-port, and the church (St Spiridon's, naturally) stands all alone on an islet at the southern tip, approached by a stone causeway. There is not much else – a couple of taverns, a shop or two, a disused cinema (every house has its TV aerial). The fishing-boats were nearly all at sea just then, but when they came back, so Arianna said, each would be moored directly outside the owner's home, some at little wooden landing-stages, some in docks cut alongside the houses.

By the time we got back to the house the luncheon party was already assembled and the food was on the table beneath the pergola – smoked mullet, shrimps, tomato with fetta cheese, lots of celery, ouzo. The company, six or seven men, rather more women, greeted me courteously; the priest I had seen on the boat, the chairman of the fishing cooperative, some miscellaneous elders and their wives. Once we were settled, they tucked into their victuals in vigorous silence. They seemed to have huge appetites. 'Now you see,' said the priest, 'what the Hav Greeks are really like.' In the city, he said, they had been oppressed for so long that they had lost their national characteristics, and had become subdued and inhibited. Evasive too, somebody said between mouthfuls. One would not know, seeing them in their poky shops and offices, that they were of a great sea-going race, a martial race – it was here after all that Achilles built his fortress, here that the Spartans created the Iron Dog! They had lost their gaiety, too and their sense of comradeship – yes, and even their ancient culture, which flourished now only on St Spiridon, whereas once, all the old historians said, Hav had been a very cradle of Hellenism. Now the city Greeks had been forced into subterfuge and secrecy. 'What you see now,' said the priest, waving his arms around the assembled company, who had fallen into rapt and solemn attention, 'is the Greekness of Hav as it always was – here alone, on our beloved island.'

After the meal they sang songs to me. Somebody fetched a mandolin, and some younger people began to dance on the terrace beneath the pergola, weaving an intricate, fairy-footed step. But happy and grateful though I was, well-fed, well-ouzo'd too, the more I watched and listened to them, somehow the less Greek those Greeks really seemed to be. There was something odd about them. Were they really Greeks at all? All the externals were there of course, clerical beard to fetta cheese, but something else, something more profound, seemed to be wrong. Their faces did not look quite like Greek faces, ancient or modern: there was a hint of something oriental to them, just the faintest suggestion of eye and cheekbone, as in the faces pictured by the old Hav portraitists. Then their bodily shape was not quite Greek either, being stringier, or tauter, or more sinewy. Their earnest ethnic loyalties seemed to me more Arab in style than Hellenic. Their ravenous appetites surprised me. Their music sounded less like melodies of Crete or Athens than of places well to the east of us, while the performance of the dancers on the terrace began to remind me uncomfortably, in its silent, deft and expressionless zeal, of tranced dervishes!

Perhaps it was the ouzo. But when they took me down to the port to catch the ferry home I happened to mention the graffiti on the hide of the Iron Dog. Out of the corner of my eye I saw Kallonia, the bishop's sister, crossing herself like the women on the ferry.

Today I mentioned these peculiar sensations to Dr Borge, as we lunched together at the Al-Asima, in the Great Bazaar. He looked at me in a penetrating way. 'You are walking on quicksands,' he said. 'I will say no more. We cannot re-write history. Nevertheless, when you have a moment take a look at a picture of the dragons on the Ishtar Gate at Babylon – not the lions, the dragons. See what you make of them.'

I went to the Athenaeum the moment we parted, and found a photograph of the dragons, proud but not vicious beasts, made of glazed brick, with jaunty serpents' tails and heads held high. I was none the wiser, though. I could see the resemblance, of course, to the Iron Dog, but so what? What could he mean? Magda says she has not the faintest idea. 'He's an old fraud anyway.' But the mystery of it, the strangeness of those Greeks, the presence of the Dog there, graffiti-scarred upon his headland, haunt me rather.

JUNE

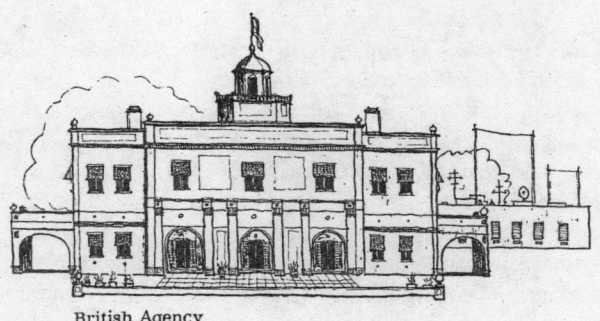

British Agency

13

At the Victor's Party

I have been into the Palace, and met the Governor. A month after the Roof-Race the winner, by then assumed to have recovered from the ordeal, is honoured at a gubernatorial garden party, the Victor's Party, which is one of the great public occasions of the Hav year. It takes no great social clout to be invited, though Signora Vattani did look rather miffed when the big official envelope, stamped rather than embossed with the Governor's emblem (a Hav bear, rampant, holding a maze-mallet) plopped through our letter-box for me. Before the war, she said, she always used to go with her husband, but of course (with a sniff) everything was so different now . . .

Long before I reached the palace gates I could hear the thump of military music over the traffic of Pendeh Square, and the party was evidently in full swing by the time I presented my invitation to the smiling sentries, and had been stentoriously announced by the footman at the door of the central salon. The Governor was there to receive his guests. 'Dirleddy, I have heard so much of your presence here. You are welcome to Hav! Allow me to introduce our guest of honour and our hero, Irfan Izmic.' Izmic looked very unlike that heap of blotched, greased and bloody flesh which had dropped from the Castle Gate four weeks before. He was in a smart tropical suit now, his hair slicked, his moustache urbanely trimmed, in his lapel the red ribbon which winners of the great contest wear until the end of their days. 'Delighted dirleddy,' said he. 'Honoured to meet you,' said I, and so I was left, as one is left at garden parties the world over, hopefully to circulate.

I was happy enough to do so. It was a grand festivity to watch. Partly in the garden, partly in the salon beneath the chandeliers, the confused society of the peninsula milled, ambled or was clotted, offering for my contemplation a splendid cross-section of *Homo hav*. The noise was considerable. Not just the military band played, resplendent in white and scarlet in the little garden bandstand, but two other musical ensembles worked away indoors. In the blue drawing-room a piano quartet, three ladies and the urbane Chinese pianist I had last seen thumping jazz in Bar 1924, played café music with much careful turnings of pages and rhythmic noddings of heads. In the pink drawing-room a folk group of six girls and six men, dressed alike in straw hats and *gallabiyehs*, performed in penetrating quarter-tones upon flutes, lutes and tambourines.

Through these varying melodies the Havians shouted to each other in their several languages, so that as I wandered through the crowd I moved from Turkish to Arabic, from Italian to Chinese to surprisingly frequent enclaves of English – for as I have discovered from the Athenaeum, Hav intellectuals in particular love to talk English among themselves. Mahmoud was there and introduced me to his hitherto unrevealed wife, who looked like a very pretty deer, but seemed to speak no known language at all. Dr Borge was there and told me to ignore the folk-artists banging and fluting away in the other room, as they were pure phonies – 'One of these evenings I'll take you to a place I know and let you hear the real thing.' Magda, in yellow, was accompanied by a handsome bearded black man, and who should be with Fatima (brown silk, helping herself to urchin mayonnaise from the buffet) but the stately figure of the tunnel pilot himself. 'I hear you have bought one of our old cars,' he said. 'A wise purchase. We keep them scrupulously.'

Presently the Governor adjourned with his guest of honour to a wide divan, covered with carpets in the Turkish way, which stood just within the french windows of the salon, looking out on to the garden. There they were joined by the Governor's wife and daughter, ample ladies both, in long white dresses and small tilted hats, who draped themselves side by side at the end of the divan, slightly separate from Izmic and His Excellency, and looked to me suggestively like odalisques. In twos and threes the citizenry took their turn to wait upon this court, and were greeted I noticed with varying degrees of condescension.

When for example athletic young men, with shy young wives, went over to grasp Izmic by the shoulder or pretend to rumple his hair, the Governor was all jollity, his ladies sweet with smiles. When elderly Turkish-looking gentlemen went, without their wives, sometimes the Governor actually rose to his feet to greet them, while his ladies adjusted their skirts and all but tidied their black hair. Others seemed less graciously received. I could not hear what was said, from my peregrinating distances, but I got the impression that sometimes the exchange of courtesies was curt. The Caliph's Wazir, though greeted by formal smiles, did not last long at the divan. A group of Greeks was all but waved away, and went off laughing rather rudely among themselves. And when Chimoun the Port Captain approached the presence with his svelte and predatory wife, I thought for a moment the Governor seemed a little nervous.

Magda and her black man, each holding a plate of langoustines, pressed me to a garden bench, in the shade of a fine old chestnut, from where I could view this intriguing pageant *in toto*. From there it all looked very colourful, very charming – the splash of crimson from the band in the corner, the bright dresses and gaudy hats, the wonderfully varied wandering wardrobe of kaftans, *gallabiyehs*, white uniforms, tight-buttoned suits and ecclesiastical headgear – and in the middle, intermittently revealed to us between the comings and goings of the guests, the Governor there on his divan, with his ladies and his champion, looking now so unmistakably Levantine that I almost expected him to pull his feet up under him and sit cross-legged on his rugs.

'I suppose you are thinking,' Magda remarked, 'what a pretty scene!' and her friend laughed cynically.

'Well it *is* a pretty scene,' I replied.

'You are so innocent,' Magda said, 'for a person of your age. You cannot have travelled much, I think. You sit here smiling around you as though it is a little show. You think it is all lobsters and urchins and nice music. Believe me it is much more than that.'

'You can say that again,' said her companion idiomatically.

'This is almost the only time in the whole year,' she went on, 'when all these people meet at the same time. Do you suppose they are here just to talk about the Roof-Race, or congratulate the Governor's daughter on her smart dress from Beirut? No, my friend, they're talking about very different things.'

'They're talking about money,' said the black man.

'Certainly,' said Magda, 'they're talking about money. And they're talking about power, and many other things too. They're not just here for fun. Look at them! Do they look as though they are having fun?'

They did actually, since half of them were stuffing urchins into their mouths, and many were laughing, and some were looking at the garden flowers, and others were deep in what seemed to be very absorbing gossip. But I saw what Magda meant. It was not exactly a *blithe* party. Currents I could not place, allusions I could not identify, seemed to loiter on the air. Separate little groups of people had assembled now, and appeared to have turned their backs on all the others. The longer I looked at the Governor the less he seemed like the benevolent figurehead of an idiosyncratic Mediterranean backwater, and the more like one of those spidery despots one reads about in old books of oriental travel, crouching there at the heart of his web.

'Well what d'you suppose they all *want*?' I asked.

'Ah,' said Magda sententiously, 'if we knew that, we would know the answer to life's riddles, wouldn't we?'

'That's for sure,' her friend added.

As I passed through the salon on my way out, having said my goodbyes to the divan ('Charmed, charmed,' murmured the two ladies, and the Governor bowed distractedly from the waist, being deep in talk with the Maronite archbishop), a man in well-cut sharkskin intercepted me. He was Mario Biancheri of the Casino. He had heard I was about, he said, and as we had friends in common in Venice, wondered if I would care to visit the Casino, which was difficult to enter without an introduction. 'You can drive out of course, but it's a terrible road – you really need four-wheel drive. But if you're prepared to get up early you could come with me in the launch one morning when we return from the market. We would see that you got home again. You would be amused? Very well, signora, it's fixed.

'By the way, did you enjoy the food? We did the catering. If you are planning to do any entertaining yourself we shall be delighted to help – we need not be as expensive as we look!' And so in the end I was seen off at the door of the palace, past the Circassian sentries, beneath the onion domes, away from the mysteries of that somewhat dream-like function, with a brisk quotation of sample prices – 'you prefer a sit-down meal? Certainly, certainly.' As I walked across the square the bands played on: thump of Souza from the garden, 'Chanson d'amour' from the blue room, and a reedy wheeze and jangle of folk melody.

14

The British Agent's name is – well, I will call him Thorne. His wife's name is – well, let us say Rosa. They are the only English residents in Hav, and he is the only foreign diplomatic representative. He keeps very much to himself. He is officially invited every year, he tells me, to the Roof-Race and the Victor's Party, but has never been to either, confining himself to private contact with the Governor or the Foreign Department when the need arises, which seems to be infrequently. He is a tall thin man, very clever I think, with a high brow and the sort of nose which, without being retroussé, slopes downwards below the nostrils to the upper lip. She was at Cambridge, where she read foreign languages, and is clever too, while affecting Kurdish jewelry and sandals with heavy gold thongs. It is touted about, naturally, that Thorne is a spy-master, and that much British and American intelligence passes through his hands: Magda says he is the original of one of John Le Carré's characters, but she can't remember which.

He is a mystery, but a mystery the people of Hav seem perfectly content to ignore. From almost anywhere on the waterfront you can see his fine white house above the harbour, radio aerials sprouting from the outbuildings behind, yet hardly anybody goes near the place, and it stands there apparently aloof to the life of the peninsula. It is a tantalizing relic of the brief and not very glorious Hav Britannica.

*

If in 1794 Nelson had obeyed his original instructions, and attacked the peninsula of Hav instead of sailing west to invest Corsica, he might never have had his eye shot out at Calvi. As it was, the British never did have to take Hav by force, for it fell into their hands peacefully under the treaty arrangements of 1815. They wanted it for strategic reasons. They were coming to see India as the true source and focus of their power, and were more and more concerned with the safety of the routes that led there. With Gibraltar already theirs, with Malta to control the central Mediterranean, the Ionians to command the Adriatic, and with Hav flying the flag away to the east, their lines of communication through the inner sea seemed to be secure.

In those days warships were small enough to make use of Hav's poor harbour, and the British promptly established a garrison, built a Residency, an Admiralty House, an Anglican church and an ice-house, and made the Protectorate of Hav and the Escarpment a proper little tight-meshed outpost of their fast coalescing empire. Many well-known imperial figures had Hav connections at one time or another. Bold General C. J. Napier, conqueror of Baluchistan, spent some months in the city reorganizing the garrison, and wrote to his wife that it was 'a dreadful hole – worse than Sind! I am sorry for the poor soldiers, but it is the price we pay for power'. The half-mad Lord Guilford, who established an Ionic university in Corfu, paid a brief spectacular visit to Hav, swathed in his usual flowing toga, to suggest a sister establishment here: it was to be called the Trojan Academy, but protests from the Sublime Porte direct to the Crown, so Guilford always claimed, put paid to the project. General Gordon was a more frequent visitor, sometimes in the course of his duties as a military engineer (he had a scheme for resuscitating the Spartan canal as a defence work), sometimes in the pursuit of Truth: just as he believed the Seychelles to be the true site of the Garden of Eden, so he was sure that Noah's Ark had really grounded on the Escarpment, and he wrote many learned papers to prove it.

Then Kinglake came of course, the then British Resident Harry Stormont having been at Eton with him; and Edward Lear painted some agreeable pictures of the castle and the Medina; and from time to time parliamentary commissions descended upon the Protectorate, as they did upon all such petty possessions, were well-fed at the

Residency, watched a smart parade of the 53rd Foot, and went home expressing the view that Her Majesty's interests on Hav were being diligently safeguarded. Frigates of the fleet put in sometimes. Garden parties were held on the Queen's birthday. An undistinguished succession of Residents came and went; the best-known was perhaps Sir Joshua Remington, who having just escaped bankruptcy by the fortunate chance of his appointment by Lord Palmerston to the office, was lampooned by *Punch*:

> *As he picked up the carver to carve,*
> *Said Sir Joshua, 'We'll never starve.*
> *For thanks to LORD P.,*
> *And the powers that be,*
> *Whatever we haven't, we've HAV.*

So for half a century the Protectorate lived the familiar life of a British overseas possession. It was not the happiest on the roster, for nearly everyone loathed it (the mosquitoes were terrible then, the drinking-water was often brackish and the food was described by Napier as being 'fit only for monkeys – if for them'). Old pictures, nevertheless, make life for the imperialists look quite bearable. We see the officers in their shakos, the ladies beneath their parasols, parading the quayside outside the Fondaco, admiring the view through telescopes from Katourian's Place, or enjoying *fêtes-champêtres* in the then empty western hills. Here in stilted sepia photographs Chinese women in wide coolie hats sell them silks and souvenirs ('Buying keepsakes in the Protectorate'), and here a visiting cricket team, very stiff at the wicket, extremely alert in the field, plays the officers of the garrison on the green outside St George's church.

Cricket continued to be played in Hav long after the end of the Protectorate; some of the Russians took it up, and as late as 1912 we read of a match between Prince Bronsky's XI and a team from Corfu. A few other British legacies died hard, too. The honorific 'Dirleddy' has been inherited, I take it, from the etiquette of the Victorian empire-builders. The version of '*Chant de doleure pour li proz chevalers qui sunt morz*' played by Missakian nowadays was arranged by a garrison bandmaster. Not only the cows and mongooses, but all the Indians one sees in Hav are migrants of the Pax Britannica – they came originally as servants and camp followers. A few places have kept their British names – China Bay, The Hook, Pyramid Rock, the triangular rock which rises out of the sea off little Yalta – and a few reactionaries still like to call the Balad 'Blacktown'.

Most of the meagre monuments of British Hav may still be identified. Westminster never put much money into the place, so that the buildings were mostly jerry-built and second-rate, but still in one form or another they have survived, their origins generally long forgotten. The Residency thrives still as the Agency – the name was adopted by agreement with the Russians in 1875, and British consuls in Hav have called themselves Agents ever since. The Anglican church however, its steeple knocked off, is now used for the storage of oil drums by the Greek fishermen, while the open space in front of it, where they used to play cricket, is now one of the market truck parks (and I have found no trace of the tombstone, mentioned in several imperial memoirs, of the officer who, 'having recently achieved his Captaincy in the Royal Engineers, Left this Station to Report to the Commander of a yet greater Corps . . .').

If you look closely at the barrack block between the Palace and the old legations you will see that its southern wing was verandahed in the Anglo-Indian manner, until the Russians stripped it of its ironwork, and the former Admiralty House, at the southern end of the Lazaretto, is now the agreeable if decrepit restaurant of the pleasure-park. As for the ice-house which stood on the eastern quay, Count Kolchok turned it into a private retreat, in whose cool chambers, if we are to believe the gossip, he often enjoyed himself with the dancer Naratlova; but it was demolished when they built the promenade of New Hav.

And one British commercial concern, out of several which made their modest fortunes from the Hav connection, is active to this day. One morning I walked into the offices of Butterworth and Sons, World-Wide Preferential Shipping Tariffs, and asked if there was actually a Mr Butterworth. Certainly there was, they said, Mr Mitko Butterworth – would I care to meet him? And there he was, the last living representative, one might say, of the Protectorate of Hav and the Escarpment – a swarthy man in his thirties, shirtsleeved below his swirling electric fan, with large gold cuff-links and round wire spectacles. Yes, he said, he was the great-great-grandson, he thought, of the Oswald Butterworth who had, in 1823, followed the flag to Hav and set up his shipping agency in that very office within the Fondaco.

Oswald had hoped, he told me, to make Hav once more the great entrepôt for the whole of the Levant trade, perhaps even the Russian trade, as British contemporaries were even then making Hong Kong the chief outlet for the wealth of China. That had never happened, but still the Butterworths had moderately prospered, outlived their several competitors, and become so much a part of Hav life that they had successfully ridden out all subsequent ebbs and flows of political circumstance.

And did he feel himself, I wondered, to be British still? He shrugged and laughed. 'When it suits me to feel British, I feel British, but it is very seldom. And rather hard. Work it out yourself. Oswald Butterworth married a Bulgarian, and there has been no new British blood in the Butterworth family since then. What am I – one thirty-secondth British?' And to my astonishment, for it seemed altogether out of character, he burst into loud song:

> 'In spite of all temptations,
> To belong to other nations,
> I remain one thirty-secondth of an E-e-e-e-nglishman!'

When Mr Thorne invited me to lunch, which he called tiffin, at the former Residency, I mentioned Mr Butterworth and his improbable command of Gilbert and Sullivan. 'Yes, I've heard about him,' the Agent said without a smile, 'but he's not a British subject. There are no British subjects here. There may be some Maltese, but they are no longer our responsibility. I have never met this Butterworth.'

'Perhaps we should invite him out, darling?' said Rosa. 'He sounds amusing.'

'I think not,' replied the Agent.

We were sitting in considerable, but somehow dullened splendour. The house was recognizably an Anglo-Indian villa, translated here from the banks of the Hooghly, but had long lost its imperial panache. The big mahogany table was handsome, but scuffed here and there. The silver was handsome too, but might have been better polished. The Indian manservant who waited on us wore a white jacket not exactly dirty, but sort of grey-looking. We ate fish with Hav cabbage, and drank white wine which I suspect to have been Cypriot. I was the only guest. 'How nice,' said Rosa, 'to see a new face. Isn't it nice, Ronald?'

'Very nice,' said Mr Thorne.

Around us on the walls were portraits of the men who had presided over the Hav Protectorate from that house – florid, well-fed Britons every one, lavishly splayed with insignia of various orders, and sometimes in military uniform. The Agent identified them all for me – 'General Ricks who made something of a fool of himself in the Crimea, Sir Joshua Remington who became Lord Remington of Hav – you may know the limerick, "Whatever we haven't we've Hav?" – Harry Stormont who was something of an artist, we have one of his paintings in the library in fact, and Sir Roland Triston, and Sir Henry Walton-Vere, the only Anglo-Indian of the lot, surprisingly enough, and Lord Hevington, and General Stockingham, and . . .'

I had hardly heard of any of them, and my mind wandered rather during this recital, concentrating instead on the fish, which was good but bony. What *were* we doing there, the Agent, his Rosa and I, eating mullet at the rubbed mahogany table from Calcutta, recalling the ineptitudes of General Ricks at Sebastopol, drinking wine we should not be drinking, in that queer little alien enclave above teeming and tumultuous Hav?

After lunch we sat on the verandah, among pots of flowering ferns, looking down to the harbour below us, where one of the salt ships was just rounding the Hook, and the Electric Ferry was slowly crossing the gap between the Lazaretto and San Pietro. I said it reminded me of Sydney. Rosa said it reminded her of the Helston river. Mr Thorne said of course the British never did quite know where they were in Hav. Sometimes they thought of it as an extension of India, sometimes as an outpost of Constantinople – 'we still call our waiters "bearers" but our watchmen "dragomans", and they always call me Sahib. "Rivers of history", one might say. You remember the quotation? No matter.'

I had heard something interesting of the house. I had heard that in 1913, when T. E. Lawrence, Lawrence of Arabia, was engaged on an archaeological excavation in Mesopotamia, he had met here the young Turkish officer Mustafa Kemal, later to be known as Attaturk.

And it is said that at this secret meeting between the Oxford don, who was a British agent, and the most formidable of the Young Turks was to have an incalculable influence upon the course of the First World War and the post-war settlement; for Attaturk is supposed to have promised that he would use his influence within the Turkish army to allow the Arab revolt, already germinating in British minds as well as Arab ones, so to succeed that in future years British influence would be paramount in the Middle East. As it turned out, Attaturk was the very Turkish commander who allowed the forces of the Arabs, under British patronage, to capture Damascus, thus ensuring British suzerainty in those parts for another forty years: if the story is true, then the white Agency above the harbour of Hav played a clandestine role of enormous significance in the history of the British Empire, of Israel, and of the world between the wars.

'I dare say,' Mr Thorne was saying, 'that you may think the survival of this Agency an anachronism. Some of my colleagues do. But our duties here have always been specialized. We are an independent window, as it were, upon the eastern Levant. Here in Hav we can make contacts denied to diplomatic missions in places closer to the mainstream. I would not like you to go away with the impression that we are merely idle lotus-eaters – that's what Kinglake called Stormont, you know, the Resident in his time – "a plump and idle lotus-eater".'

'No, plump we may be,' interjected Rosa, who is, 'but idle certainly not. Lucky old Stormont hadn't got a radio link, had he?'

The conversation moved on, by way of Wales and the British monarchy, to the subject of 24 Residenzstrasse. 'I hope you don't believe all the bizarre things they say about it,' said Mr Thorne quite crossly. 'Von Tranter was as thorough a Nazi as anyone else, I can assure you, and worked hand-in-glove with von Papen throughout the war. Putting up that plaque was a disgrace. As for the poppycock about Hitler coming to Hav, believe me, if he had ever been within a hundred miles of this Agency, he would never have got home alive.'

It seemed a good moment, as we appeared to have entered cloak-and-dagger territory, to raise the story of Lawrence and Attaturk. This was evidently unwelcome. 'Lawrence did come to this house,' said the Agent, in a formal tone of voice, 'but the visit was purely private. He came as the guest of the then Agent, a somewhat eccentric man called Winchester, the first man in Hav, as a matter of fact, to ride a motor-cycle. His interest was in the barrow-graves of the salt-marsh, at that time supposed to be Minoan, now known to be troglodytic. He stayed some ten days, and then proceeded overland to his dig in Iraq. Anything else you may have heard,' said Mr Thorne conclusively, 'is totally unfounded.' Thus on a detectably minatory note the Agent's hospitality came to an end, and with 'So lovely to see a new face' from Rosa, and 'You must come again some time' from Mr Thorne – 'how long did you say you were staying?' – I was shown to my car and waved fairly perfunctorily down the drive.

Hardly was I around the corner and in the shrubbery, out of sight of the house, when an elderly man in green *gallabiyeh* and turban urgently signalled me to stop. 'Excuse me, memsahib,' he said, 'I am head dragoman here. Bearer says you ask about Lawrence Pasha – I tell you truth now. My father was dragoman here then, and he remembered visit of Lawrence Pasha very well. Now I tell you, *at same time Turkish gentleman stayed in this house*. Mr Thorne not tell you that I think. British prefer to forget that. But my father remember very well, and he knew who that Turkish gentleman was, *he knew* . . . He remembered very clearly, and many times he described to us Lawrence Pasha riding Winchester Sahib's motorcycle up and down this drive. He never rode motorcycle before, but very fast he rode, very very fast, very dangerous: and once, my father said, that Turkish gentleman went for ride on back seat of motorbike, and when they came back to this house he was very pale.'

I have asked several people at the Athenaeum what they know of the Lawrence story, but they do not seem very interested, just as they see nothing to be wondered at in the fact that the fishermen's oil store used to be an English church, and seem indifferent to the presence of the white house with its radio masts above the harbour. 'All I want from Britain is the Beatles,' Magda said to me one day: for their tastes in western music are years behind the times.

15

To Casino Cove – dreaming? – a call from Dodo – hard and steely – Solveig and the champagne – a remarkable menu

It was the loveliest of pearly mornings, all warm and still, the sea as calm as urchin soup, the castle shimmering in the warm sun behind us, when Mario Biancheri, his Chinese henchmen and I scudded away from the market quay on the day of my initiation into Casino Cove.

Nothing else was moving on the water, but all around us, as we swept in a wide showy curve from the waterfront, the city was awakening. The first traffic was just entering Pendeh Square, on the New Hav promenade somebody was doing callisthenics, and the gardener was already up and about in the flower-beds of the British Agency. At the coal wharf a coaster was unloading in a haze of sooty dust. I sat in the stern of the boat, and thought that Hav had never looked so lovely – gone all its seediness, all its decay, from this perspective, on such a morning! Round the Hook we swept, and the hills rose green and fresh on either side, and under the Conveyor Bridge, whose platform was swinging, entirely untenanted except for the captain, from one tower to the other – and there was the Iron Dog glaring down at us from the headland, and before us the open sea, veiled in a thin morning haze, stretched away to Cyprus and distant Africa.

It looked an entirely open sea – as so often, Hav felt utterly alone in the world. But when we had rounded the southern point, passed through the St Spiridon channel, and entered the wide declivity called China Bay, busy life began to show – and life altogether separate from that of the city we had left behind us. It was like entering a different ocean. There were scores of Chinese fishing craft about, their crews grimly working at nets or riggings. There were marker buoys everywhere, and schools of those apparently abandoned boats, silently bobbing, which give a particular mystery to every Chinese shore. Sometimes Biancheri waved at the fishermen, but they responded only in an abstracted Chinese way: once our helmsman shouted something, but nobody answered.

Straggling over its hillocks now I could see Yuan Wen Kuo, brown and huddled, and then we were around the next point, and before us on a tight little cove, hemmed about by steep cliffs, thickly greened by woods, half-obscured by the masts and upperworks of a dozen large yachts, stood the buildings of the Casino. They did not look like Hav at all. They were low, and pink-washed, and had pale tiled roofs, and seemed to breathe, even at that distance, the very *numen* of immense wealth. Biancheri caught my eye and made a face, wry, amused, half-apologetic, implying 'well, there we are, for what it's worth . . .' I shouted a response above the din of the engines. 'Breakfast should be good,' I said.

Breakfast was. The hotel was still asleep, so Biancheri and I ate alone upon the wide restaurant verandah, with its yellow-cushioned furniture, its bright flowering plants, its apparently numberless and weightless Chinese servants, the yachts gleaming across the lawn and the lovely cove beyond. Biancheri laughed to see me, as the steaming coffee arrived with cornflakes and Oxford marmalade. 'You think you are dreaming? But there's no *Times*! What a shame! We must complain to the management!'

Presently the management joined us, in the elegantly suited and delicately after-shaved person of Monsieur Tomas Chevallaz, a Swiss, he told me, who had worked in his time at the Mandarin Hong Kong, the Connaught in London and 'a pub of my own at home'. The Hav Casino, he told me, was quite different from them all. It was unique. Since its beginnings in the late 1920s it had never had to advertise – all was by word of mouth, or by inheritance. Now it was a private club, and as old Pierpont Morgan remarked about the owning of steam yachts, if you had to ask how much it cost, you couldn't afford it. 'In the twelve years I have managed this place, I can remember only about a dozen of our guests who did *not* arrive on their own yachts.'

He identified some of the boats lying there below us – this one a Spanish industrialist's, that one a shipowner's, another the matrimonially disputed property of an American actor – and by now a few of the guests were trickling on to the terrace for their breakfasts. Most of them slept very late, Chevallaz said, having been up most of the night at the gaming tables; and some of them, as everyone knew, preferred to sleep the sleep narcotic, which is why he would be grateful if I did not mention present guests by name – 'in Hav nobody minds, it is when they get home to their boardrooms . . .'

Those who did appear looked anything but drugged. They were the lean, lithe kind, smooth-tanned, and had probably already played a game of tennis, or been swimming, or at least gone for a jog through the trees. They all seemed to know each other intimately, and exchanged greetings across the tables in variously accented English – 'You're looking rather terrific' – 'My dear, I had a call from Dodo' – or, 'Kurt says he's never going to eat urchins again'. They seemed to me nation-less and quite timeless. They might have been from any decade of our century, or earlier. They were the stuff of Carlsbad, Newport, Monte Carlo in the thirties, even Hav itself in the days of the Russians. 'Have you heard from Scott?' they asked each other. '*What* a pity Otto isn't here!'

'You see,' said Chevallaz as we walked over the sprinkled lawns to his office, 'our clients are different from others. They cannot fly to Hav. They can hardly drive. They would be mad to come by train. They can really only come in their own ships, or their friends' ships, and that's what makes them feel like rich people from other times. You are quite right. And when they are here, here they stay. As you know, they're not encouraged to take their yachts into the city harbour, where they'd probably sink, and it's a frightful track over the cliffs here. Why move? I doubt if one of our guests in a thousand ever goes into the city, and we much prefer it that way.'

All around his office were portraits of the Casino's famous guests. There were kings, statesmen, authors, bankers, actresses, great ladies of the social circuit. There was Noël Coward – 'To dear André – happy days!' – and there was Hemingway in a bush shirt – 'To Hav . . .?'. Coco Chanel was fuzzed and misty, in the photographic style of the day. Maurice Chevalier was wearing his boater. Winston Churchill painted on the beach. Thomas Mann looked haggard. And no, could it be –? 'Yes, I'm afraid so, though I'm not sure he ought to be there. He is supposed to have come to Hav, you know, secretly during the war, and legend says he was picked up by a U-boat at the cove here. We don't know the truth, but my predecessor hung the picture there anyway. I'm often told I should remove it, but I don't know . . . he's not the only villain on the wall.'

His mother loved him anyway, I suggested. 'In that case he did *not* come here,' Biancheri said. 'Nobody who comes to the Hav Casino ever had a mother.' It is clearly not a place rich in the milk of human kindness, and as we wandered around that morning, from pool to solarium, from kitchens to gambling rooms, something very hard and steely seemed to impregnate the air. Almost everyone who works at the Cove is Chinese, and the responses we got from the staff were taciturn, just as the buildings themselves, fitted out in every last degree of luxury, seemed nevertheless devoid of comfort. Above the roulette tables Chevallaz showed me the hidden mirrors and monitors which ensure that the billionaires below do not cheat (not that any of them try – they are much too clever for that). In the restaurant he showed me the one-way mirrors behind which less exhibitionist celebrities prefer to dine – seeing but unseen.

Wherever we went young Chinese in olive-green fatigues seemed to be prowling around holding night-sticks. 'Please don't ask me,' said Chevallaz, 'if they have guns too.' Security, he said, was one of his chief headaches, especially as so many of his guests brought their own bodyguards too – 'see that guy over there?' – and leaning against the wall of one of the bungalows was a tall heavy man in white tennis gear, holding a walkie-talkie and looking distinctly bulged around the hips. There had been sufficient mayhem at the Cove in its time, Chevallaz said – did I know about the Tiananmen affair? No? Ah well, it was a subject he preferred to stay clear of anyway. 'I'm only an employee, and I like my job.'

And who were his employers? Oh, the same Chinese syndicate, *mutatis mutandis*, that had founded the Casino back in the 1920s. All the money was Chinese – well, almost all – he had heard some European money had slid in, one way or another, after the war. And the Hav government – it had no share? Better not know, he implied.

*

'*Jan*, my dear,' came a loud deep voice from a patio. It was Solveig, a Swedish actress of my acquaintance, so Chevallaz left us together – 'I'll send coffee over,' he said.

'Jan, how amazing, of all people! You're alone? God, I wish I were, but you know how Eric is, he's so terribly friendly with everyone, and here we are stuck in this absurd place.'

'You don't like it?'

'Darling, how could one? It's absurd, obscene. Nothing but millionaires and Chinese people everywhere, and gambling – you know I hate gambling. I suppose you're living in some delicious garret somewhere. You *are* lucky. Sit down at once, sit here, tell me everything!'

I told her about Signora Vattani and my apartment in New Hav, and about the harbour, and the onion-domed Serai, and the snow raspberries, and Missakian's trumpet, and the Athenaeum, and Brack and Kretev. How absolutely perfect, she cried, she could hardly wait to see it all for herself. How could she get into Hav? Well, I said, I supposed she could get hold of a jeep or something to get her up the cliff-track, and down the edge of the salt-marsh, and through the Balad; or alternatively she might persuade Signor Biancheri to take her on the market launch, though that meant getting up at about three in the morning.

At that moment the coffee arrived, together with a bunch of fresh roses, a bottle of champagne and a bowl of fruit. 'When you have enjoyed your coffee,' said a note in Chevallaz's fastidious hand, 'I hope you will drink my health in something a little stronger.' Tacitly we abandoned Solveig's visit to Hav. 'What a marvellous man Chevallaz is,' she said. 'Marvellous,' I agreed, 'and he knows his business, too.'

'There is somebody else here you may know,' said Biancheri, showing me into the bar, and sure enough, the moment I saw the face of the head barman, I remembered him from Venice. Seeing his bitter-sweet smile there, reaching across the bar to shake his hand, gave me a most curious sense of *déjà vu*. And when I looked around the cramped but indefinably expensive little saloon, too, all seemed creepily familiar to an old habituée of Harry's Bar: the same sorts of faces, the same loud talk, the same confident laughter, the same weather-eye on the door to see if anyone who matters is coming in.

'But not,' said Biancheri, joining me with a gin-fizz in a corner of the room – 'not *altogether* the same food that you are accustomed to get from Ciprianis. I think you will agree that our restaurant menu is something a little different.' He was right. Could there be such a menu, I wondered, anywhere else on earth? Not only were there the old stalwarts of classical French and Italian cooking – not only the inescapable pigeons' breasts and raw mushrooms of the cuisine nouvelle – not only roast beef for traditionalists, jellied duck for Sinophiles, bortsch for nostalgia, couscous, pumpkin pie – there was also a fascinating selection of Hav specialities.

You could eat sea-urchins grilled, meunière, baked, stewed, in batter, with ginger garnish, as a pâté, in an omelette, in a soup or raw. You could eat roast kid in the escarpment style, which meant cold with a herb-flavoured mayonnaise, or barbecued over catalpa charcoal from the western hills. You could eat the legs of frogs from the salt-marshes, which are claimed to have a flavour like no others, or Hav eels, which are pickled in rosemary brine, or the pink-coloured mullet which is said to be unique to these waters, and which the Casino likes to serve smoked with dill sauce, or the tall sweet celery which grows on the island of the Greeks, or a salad made entirely, in the inexplicable absence of lettuce anywhere on the peninsula, of wild grasses and young leaves gathered every morning in the hills above Yuan Wen Kuo. You could even eat a dish, otherwise undefined, listed as *ours hav faux*.

This was only a joke, said Biancheri, though in the 1920s Hav bear really was eaten sometimes at the Casino. Now the false bear was no more than a bear-shaped duck terrine. 'But then,' he added, 'it is all a joke. For myself I prefer scrambled eggs.'

I did not stay for lunch, anyway. As the hungrier plutocrats began to drift out of the bar towards the restaurant, Biancheri walked down with me to the waiting launch, where the boatswain started up his engines as he saw us approaching, and the deckhand untied the hawser to push off. 'You will find something to sustain you on the way home,' said Biancheri, 'in the after cabin': and so as we splashed and sprayed our way back to Hav I sat in the stern like Waring, laughing, and eating bread, cheese, apples and Greek celery, washed down with ice-cold retsina. The Chinese bowed soundlessly when I stepped ashore beneath the Fondaco.

16

Hav and the maze – artistic cross-breeding – on poetry – on pictures – on music – Avzar Melchik – honouring an emblem

You may wonder what a maze-mallet is, such as appears in the paws of the bear on the Governor's emblem, and why a maze should be configured on the fretwork of the House of the Chinese Master. Forgive me. The maze is so universal a token of Hav, appears so often in legends and artistic references of all kinds, that one comes to take it for granted.

The idea of the maze has always been associated with Hav. The first reference to a Hav maze-maker comes in Pliny, who says the greatest master of the craft 'lived in the peninsula called by the people of those parts Hav, which some say means the place of summer, but others the place of confusions'. An ancient tradition says that the great labyrinth of Minoan Crete, in whose bowels the Minotaur lived, was made not by Daedalus, as the Greeks had it, but by the first and greatest of the Hav maze-makers, Avzar, who was kidnapped from the peninsula and blinded when his work was done: it is perhaps this remote fable that encouraged archaeologists, for many years, to suppose a Minoan connection in Hav, and to claim traces of Cretan design in the fragmentary remains of its acropolis.

Later it used to be said that the whole of the salt-flats, with their mesh of channels, conduits and drying-basins, were originally nothing more than a gigantic maze, fulfilling some obscure ritual purpose, and of course it has been repeatedly suggested that the caves of the Kretevs, which have never been scientifically explored, are not really caves at all, but only the visible entrances of an artificial labyrinth riddling the whole escarpment. How proper it seemed to Russian romantics, that the Hav tunnel should spiral upon itself so mazily within the limestone mass!

There is an innocuous little maze of hedges and love-seats in the Governor's garden, and one or two are rumoured to be hidden within the courtyard walls of houses in the Medina. Otherwise there are no Hav mazes extant, and for that matter none historically confirmable from the past. Yet the spirit of the maze has always fascinated the people of Hav, and the tokens of the maze-maker, as they have been fancifully transmitted down the ages, are inescapable in the iconography of the city: the mallet, with which Avzar at the beginning of time beat his iron labyrinth into shape, the honeycomb which is seen as a natural type of the maze, the bull-horns which are doubtless a vestige of the supposed Minoan link.

Some scholars go further, and say that the conception of the maze has profoundly affected the very psyche of Hav. It certainly seems true that if there is one constant factor binding the artistic and creative centuries together, it is an idiom of the impenetrable. The writers, artists and musicians of this place, though they have included few native geniuses, have seldom been obvious or conventional. They have loved the opaque more than the specific, the intuitive more than the rational. Pliny said they wrote in riddles, and declared their sculptures to be like nothing so much as lumps of coral. Manet on the other hand, visiting Hav as a young man in 1858, wrote to his mother: 'I feel so much at home in this city, among these people, whose vision is so much less harsh than that of people in France, and whose art looks as though it has been gently smudged by rain, or blurred by wood-smoke.'

For myself I suspect this lack of edge has nothing to do with mazes, but is a result of Hav's ceaseless cross-fertilization down the centuries. Hardly has one manner of thought, school of art, been absorbed than it is overlaid by another, and the result, as Manet saw, is a general sense of intellectual and artistic pointillism – nothing exact, nothing absolute, for better or for worse. You can see it at the museum in the folk-art of the peninsula, which is a heady muddle of motifs eastern and western, realist and symbolical, practical and mystically unexplained; and you can see it all around you in the architecture.

The Arab buildings of Hav, for instance, were less purely Arab than any others of their age. It was not just a matter of incorporating classical masonries into their buildings, as often happened elsewhere: the Corinthian columns of Hav's Grand Mosque were made by the Arabs themselves, and on many of the tall merchant houses of the Medina you may see classical pilasters and even architraves, besides innumerable eaves and marble embellishments derived from the House of the Chinese Master. The one great Chinese building in the peninsula is a mish-mash of architectural allusions. The British built their Residency as if they were in India. And we have seen already with what adaptive flair architects Schröter and Huhn, when the time came, mixed their metaphors of Hav. It is the way of the place – rivers of history! You remember the quotation?

Very early in Hav's history the arts began to show symptoms of cultural confusion. 'The language of these people,' Marco Polo wrote, 'which is generally that of the Turks, contains also words and phrases of unknown origin, peculiar to hear.' They were, linguists have only recently come to realize, words of the troglodytic language, a fragile offshoot of the Celtic.

The earliest known poet of Hav was the Arab Rahman ibn Muhammed, 'The Song-Bird', who lived in the thirteenth century: in his work occur words, inflexions, ideas and even techniques (including the alliterative device called *cynghanedd*) which seem to show that in those days a Celtic poetic tradition was still very much alive in this peninsula. It has even been lately suggested that Rahman may have been in touch with his contemporary on the far side of Europe, the Welsh lyric bard Dafydd ap Gwilym. Here in Professor Morris David's translation are some lines from the Song-Bird's poem 'The Grotto':

> *Ah, what need have we of mosque*
> *Or learned imam,*
> *When into the garden of our delights*
> *Flies the sweet dove of Allah's mercy*
> *With her call to prayer?*

And here in my own translation is part of Dafydd ap Gwilym's poem 'Offeren y Llwyn', 'The Woodland Mass':

There was nothing there, by great God
Anything but gold for the chancel roof . . .
And the eloquent slim nightingale,
From the corner of the grove nearby,
Wandering poetess of the valley, rang to the multitude
The Sanctus bell, clear its trill,
And raised the Host
As far as the sky . . .

Coincidence? Or perhaps, more probably than actual communication between the two poets, some empathy of temperament and tradition. Celtic words had disappeared from the Hav poetic vocabulary by the seventeenth century, but still the poet Gamal Misri was writing of the natural world in a way quite unknown among other Muslim poets of the day, and dealing with religious matters in idioms astonishingly close to those of his contemporaries far away on the western Celtic fringe – idioms that would have cost him dear in Egypt, Persia or Iraq. This is his startling evocation of the Attributes of Allah, again in David's version:

He can see as doth the Telescope, to the furthest Stars.
He knows of the ways of man as the Compass knoweth the Pole.
He doth create Gold from Dross as doth the Alchemist,
And as the great Advocate doth argue for us before the Courts of
   Eternity . . .

Visual artists, too, even in the great days of Islamic Hav, did not hesitate to risk the disapproval of the faithful by painting living portraits – not simply stylized representations, such as you find in Persian miniatures, but formal portraits of real people, sitting to be painted as they would in the west. The so-called Hav-Venetian school of painting, which flourished throughout the sixteenth century, was unique, producing the only such genre in the Islamic world, and there are no examples of its work outside Hav. Even in the city they are very rare. A few are thought to be in private hands, but the only specimens on public display are five hanging in the former chapel of the Palace, which is open to the public at weekends. They are very strange. Large formal oil-paintings of merchants and their wives, dressed in the Venetian style but looking unmistakably Havian with their rather Mongol cheeks and hard staring eyes, their painters are unknown, and they are signed simply with illegible ciphers and the Islamic date. They are hardly, I think, great works of art. They look as though they have been painted by not terribly gifted oriental pupils at the atelier of Veronese, say, being very rich in colour and detail (pet terriers, mirrors, the House of the Chinese Master in one background, the harbour islands in another) but queerly lifeless in effect. I suspect myself that the artists were Chinese, for they remind me of paintings done for European clients in Canton in the eighteenth century, though their technique is far more sophisticated and their subjects are altogether more sumptuous. The Havians are immensely proud of them, and forbid their copying or reproduction – but that may be only a relic of the days when their very existence was kept a secret, lest Islamic zealots harm them.

I really do not think Havians excel at the musical art. They are adept enough at western forms, and addicted to Arabic pop, but the indigenous kinds seem to me less than thrilling. Dr Borge was as good as his word, and took me last week to the 'place he knew', which turned out to be a dark café in one of those morose unpaved streets of the Balad, between the railway line and the salt-flats. Here, he said, the very best of Hav folk-music was to be heard. The night we went the performers were a particular kind of ensemble called *hamshak*, 'sable', because they specialized in elegiac music, and this made for a melancholy evening. They were all men, dressed in hooded monk-like cloaks supposed to be derived from the habits of Capuchin confessors who came here with the Crusaders. Their instruments were rather like those of the folk-music group at the Victor's Party, only more so: reedier, wheezier, janglier still, and given extra density by two drummers beating drums made of furry animal skins ('Hav bear skins,' said Dr Borge – 'no, I am only joking'). We drank beer, we ate grilled fish with our fingers, and through the sombre light of the place the music beat at us. Sometimes, apparently without pattern, one or another of the musicians broke into a sad falsetto refrain ('reminiscent isn't it,' said the young doctor, 'of *cante hondo*?') Sometimes, in the Arab way, the music suddenly stopped altogether and there was a moment of utter silence before the whole band erupted once more in climactic unison.

It was more interesting than enjoyable. It *was* rather like *cante hondo*, having sprung I suppose from the same musical roots. But the clatter of the tambourines and the clash of the cymbals reminded me irresistibly of Chinese music, such as one endures during the long awful hours of the Beijing Opera, while the plaintive notes of the flutes seem to come from some other culture entirely. Could it be, I wondered, that in Hav music, as in Hav medieval poetry, some dim Celtic memory is at work? Anything was possible, the Philosopher said; and when after the performance I put the same question to the band leader, a suitably cadaverous man with an Abraham Lincoln beard, his eyes lit up in a visionary way. 'Often I feel it,' he said, 'like something very cold out of the long ages' – a sufficiently convincing phrase, I thought, to catch his inspiration's meaning.

Out of the long ages certainly comes the genius of Avzar Melchik, the best-known Hav writer of the twentieth century, whose personality I can most properly use to cap this brief digression into criticism. If there is nothing overtly Celtic in his work, there is much that is undeniably mazy – even the given name he adopted, you may notice, is that of the great maze-man of legend.

Melchik, who died in 1955 (the year in which he was tipped as a likely rival to Haldór Laxness for the Nobel Literature Prize), wrote in Turkish and in French, and sometimes in both at the same time, alternating passages and even sentences between the languages. He was never in the least Europeanized, though – Armand dismisses him as a mere provincial – and his novels, if you can call them novels, are all set in Hav. They are powerful evocations of the place, through which there wander insubstantial characters, figures of gossamer, drifting for ever through the Old City's alleys or along the waterfront. Melchik so detested the invention of New Hav that he refused to recognize its existence in his art, and though his stories are set in the 1940s and 1950s, the Hav that they inhabit is essentially Count Kolchok's Hav, giving them all a haunting sense of overlap.

There is no doubt that Melchik was obsessed by the idea of the maze. Every one of his books is really its diagram. But in his most famous work, and the only one widely known in the West, he turns the conception inside out. *Bağlılık* ('Dependence') is the tale of a woman whose life, very gently and allusively described, is a perpetual search not for clarity but for complexity. She feels herself to be vapidly self-evident, her circumstances banal, and so she deliberately sets out to entangle herself. But when at last she feels she is released from her simplicities – has reached the centre of the maze in fact – she finds to her despair that her last state is more prosaic than her first.

Soon after finishing *Bağlılık* Melchik died. He was unmarried, and lived a life of supreme simplicity himself in a small wooden house, hardly more than a hut, on the edge of the Balad. It is now kept up as a little shrine, with the writer's pens still on his desk, his coat still hanging behind the door, and beside the china wash-basin, for all the world as though he has just been called into another room, the copy of Pascal's *Pensées* which he is said to have been reading on the last day of his life. An elderly woman acts as caretaker, paid by the Athenaeum, and told me when I visited the house that she felt the shade of Melchik ever-present there. 'When I make myself a cup of coffee in the kitchen, I often feel I should make one for him too.'

'And do you like this ghost?'

She thought for a moment before she replied. 'Have you been to his grave?' she asked. 'Perhaps that will answer the question for you.'

So I went there. Melchik was a Maronite Christian, and he is buried in the Maronite cemetery behind the power station. His grave is not hard to find – it stands all by itself at the northern corner within a hedge of prickly pears. You can see nothing of it, though, so formidable is this surrounding barrier, until you are within a few feet: and then you find it to be, not a slab, or a cross, or an obelisk, but a twisted mass of iron, like a half-unravelled ball of metallic wool, mounted on a stone slab with the single word MELCHIK just visible within the tangle. He designed it himself.

I saw what the caretaker meant. Could one exactly *like* such a spirit? Nothing, I thought, so cut-and-dried: but even there, all the same, where Melchik was represented only by those crude bold letters within the meshed and worried metal, I felt his presence burning.

Few places, I must say, honour their emblems more loyally than Hav honours its generic and imaginary maze. This city may not look especially labyrinthine, but behind its façades, I am coming to realize, beneath its surfaces bold, bland or comical, there lie a myriad passages unrevealed. Perhaps even the subterranean short cuts of the Roof-Race enthusiasts are only allegorical really!

Of course all cities have their hidden themes and influences – New York has its Mob, Rome its Christian Democrats, London its Old Boy Network, Singapore its Triads, Dublin its Republican Army, all working away there, out of sight and generally out of thought, to determine the character of the place. The unseen forms of Hav, though, seem to me harder to define than any, so vague are they, so insidious, and I find it difficult to enunciate the feeling this is beginning to leave in my mind. It is a tantalizing and disquieting sensation. It is rather like the taste you get in the butter, if it has been close to other foods in the refrigerator; or like the dark calculating look that cats sometimes give you; or the sudden silence that falls when you walk into a room where they are talking about you; or like one of those threadbare exhausting dreams that have you groping through an impenetrable tangle of time, space and meaning, looking for your car keys.

JULY

Castle Gate, Medina

17

High summer is on us, and I see why the British loathed the Protectorate so. 'Oh what a foretaste of hell this is,' poor Napier wrote home to his wife, and he was accustomed to the miseries of Karachi. It is not merely that Hav is hot – it is no hotter than anywhere else in the eastern Mediterranean – nor even that it is particularly humid. The trouble is an oppressive sensation of enclosure, a dead-end air, which can make one feel horribly claustrophobic.

They say the suicide rate is high, and I am not surprised. When I look out from my terrace now the citizenry below looks all but defeated – prostrate on park benches, or shuffling dejectedly along the pavements beneath floppy straw hats and parasols. Out in the Balad, where there are no trees, and not much greenery either, it is far worse; the dust lies thickly in those pot-holed streets, the shacks with their iron roofs are like ovens, and the people sprawl about like so many corpses, beneath shelters rigged up of poles and old canvas.

There is no air-conditioning in Hav, except at the Casino (and perhaps a few very rich houses of Medina and Yuan Wen Kuo). We depend still upon revolving fans, upon wind towers, upon the shades and awnings which now cover every window, and in the Palace at least, upon electrically operated punkahs – huge sheets of tasselled canvas waving ponderously about to stir a little fitful breeze through the stifling salons. Those massed fans are twirling desperately now beneath the high ceilings of the Serai, but even so, Hav being Hav, many of the more senior clerks take all their files into the gardens, and are to be seen scattered over the brown dry grass with their documents spread around them and thermos flasks close to hand. Signora V spends most of the day sitting on the roof reading old magazines, and the urchin soup at the Fondaco café is served chilled, like a very exotic vichyssoise.

The English hated it; and yet there is to the flavour of this stagnant city, limp and hangdog in the heat, something peculiarly seductive, rather like that smell of rotting foliage you sometimes discover in the depths of woodlands – a fungus smell, sweet and dangerous. It is a curious fact that of the exiles who have come in modern times to spend a few weeks, a few months in Hav, nearly all have come in the summer time, when the city is at its cruellest.

Armand is of course the expert on Hav's exiles, and in the heat of noon the other day, as we drank lime juice at the little refreshment stall which has sprung up on the promenade, I asked him how he accounted for this odd preference.

'It is simple.' (Everything is simple to Armand Sauvignon.) 'Hav is like some exile itself, and never more so than in these terrible days of July and August. *Ergo*, like goes to like, and your wandering poet, your dreaming philosopher, your Freud or your Wagner feels most at home here when everything is at its worst.'

'Drinking iced lime juice,' said I, 'beneath a sunshade on the promenade.'

'Ha! *Touché!* But they did not always live like us!'

Nor did they. By and large the Hav exiles have lived anonymously, or at least obscurely, during their time in the city. I went one day to the apartment in which Freud had his lodgings, when he came to Hav in 1876 to search for the testes of the eel. Seconded by the Department of Comparative Anatomy at Vienna University, he had already failed in this task at Trieste, but the Hav eel has the reputation of extreme virility, frequenting as it does the irrigation canals and brackish pools of those aphrodisiac salt-marshes, so he transferred his researches here. The newly installed Russian administration allowed him to use as a laboratory the old ice-house, not yet converted to Count Kolchok's purposes, and he found himself lodgings in the House of the Chinese Master.

To my surprise I discovered that he is remembered there still. Clambering up the spiral staircase, now strewn with litter and scratched with incomprehensible slogans, I found the eighth floor, in Freud's time one big apartment, divided into four tenements; but when I knocked at the first door, and asked if this was where the scientist had stayed, 'Yes,' said at once the tousle-haired young woman who opened the door, 'come in and see.' It was an ungainly room she showed me – wedge-shaped, with only a narrow wall at the inner end, and a single window at the other looking through the marble mesh outside to the roofs of the Great Bazaar – and it was in a state of homely chaos, which the woman casually did her best to reduce, picking up clothes and papers from the floor as we entered, and clearing a pile of sewing from the sofa to give us sitting space.

'It was my great-grandmother's place then – she was Austrian, she came here as governess to a Russian family, but married a local man. Of course Freud was unknown in those days, and nobody took much notice of him. It was only in my father's time that people began to be interested.'

'Lots of people come to see the place?'

'Lots? Not lots. Perhaps seven or eight a year. Sometimes they are interested in Freud, sometimes in eels! My husband does not welcome them, but then it was my family that Sigmund lived with, not his.'

'Sigmund!' I laughed. 'You know him well!'

'Yes, yes, I feel I do. He is very kindly remembered in our family – such a nice young man, we were always told, with his funny stories and his jokes. Besides, we have little things of his here that bring him close to me' – and opening a drawer she brought out a black leather box, embossed S.F., and showed me its quaint contents. There was a comb – 'Freud's comb?' 'Sigmund's comb, certainly' – and a silver-gilt pen, and a letter from the Trieste laboratory of the comparative anatomy department wishing him luck – '*After 400 Trieste eels, my dear old boy, you deserve to find your quarry among the salts of Hav*' – and a silhouette in an oval frame which portrayed, she said, Freud's mother. 'And here,' she said, 'is a funny rhyme that

Sigmund left for my great-grandmother when he went away.' It was four lines of German, in a clear script, which I will try to translate into verse:

> *To my dear Frau Makal:*
> *If you find, upon eating an eel,*
> *A part [körperteil] you would rather avoid,*
> *Please pack up that bit of your evening meal*
> *And send it to young Dr Freud.*

For poor Freud, having dissected those 400 eels in Trieste, examined another 200 during his six weeks in Hav, and never did find a testes – a curious failure, remarks his biographer Ernest Jones, for the inventor of the castration complex!

It was historical chance, of course, that brought Anastasia to Hav in the height of summer – if indeed she came at all. Of all this city's exiles, voluntary or compulsory, real or legendary, she is the one Hav most enjoys talking about, partly because people here are still enthralled by the Russian period of their history, but chiefly because romance says her vast collection of jewelry is still hidden somewhere in the peninsula.

As to whether she really came, opinions vary. Count Kolchok swore to the end of his days that she did not, and Anna Novochka also denies it: pure tosh, she says – 'if she was ever here, would I not have known of it?' On the other hand there is a strong tradition in the Yeğen family that in August 1918 a girl arrived on the train in a sealed coach, all curtains drawn, together with three servants and a mountain of baggage – to be met at the frontier by a car from the Serai, while the baggage was picked up by mule-cart at the central station and taken to the western hills.

Others say Anastasia arrived on board a British warship, which anchored beyond the Iron Dog and sent her in by jolly-boat, while wilder stories suggest she struggled by foot over the escarpment, helped by Kretevs – even living for a time, so it was imagined in a recent historical novel, in one of their caves. I often meet people who claim that their parents met her, though never it seems in very specific circumstances, only at some ball or other, or at the railway station. There is a legend that she was at Kolchok's funeral – and a fable, inevitably perhaps, that she succeeded Naratlova as his mistress.

But nobody offers any very definite theories as to what became of her. Perhaps she went on to America? Perhaps, when Russian rule ended in Hav, she simply faded into the White Russian community here, adopting another name as Anna did? Perhaps she was murdered by the KGB? Perhaps she is still alive? Far more substantial are speculations about her treasure, which seems to have grown over the years until it now sometimes embraces most of the Russian crown jewels. The existence of this trove is taken very seriously. The Palace with its outbuildings has been combed and combed again. Little Yalta, a very popular site, has almost been taken apart. Every weekend you see people with metal detectors setting off for the derelict villas of the western hills, and Anna has a terrible time keeping intruders out of her garden – 'and I ask you, if there was treasure in my flower-beds would I be living like this?'

I have an open mind about Anastasia, but it is intriguing to think that, if she really did escape to Hav, her exile might well have overlapped with that of Trotsky, who spent a secretive month here in the summer of 1929. This is well-documented. He was photographed arriving on the train (the picture hangs in the pilot's office), and he lived in an old Arab house just within the Castle Gate of the Medina – hardly a stone's throw from the Palace compound so recently vacated by Kolchok and his Czarist apparatus. Melchik has described the arrangements in his novel *Dönüş* ('The Return'): the gunmen always on the flat roof of the house, the heavy steel shutters which closed off the central courtyard in case of a siege. When Trotsky went out, which was very rarely it seems, he was hemmed all about by bodyguards; when he left for France, at the start of the fateful wanderings that led him in the end to Mexico, it is said he departed on board a private yacht. The house is now occupied by a Muslim craft school, and the only reminders of Trotsky's stay are the shutters still attached to the courtyard pillars – very reassuring, the headmaster told me waggishly, when pupils show signs of rebelling.

It has been suggested that Hitler's probably apocryphal visit to Hav may have been sparked by Wagner's paradoxical fondness for the place. Paradoxical because there seems to me nothing remotely Wagnerian about Hav, and its summer discomforts (the composer's three stays were all in July) do not seem at all to his taste.

He was apparently compelled, though, by the brooding wall of the escarpment, by the mysterious anachronism of the Kretevs in their high caverns, and by the idea that in Hav the Celtic gods of the old European pantheon had somehow found their last apotheosis. He lived here in conditions of heroic austerity – none of his habitual silks and velvet hangings – in a wooden house near the railway station, burnt down during the fire of 1927 which also destroyed the Cathedral of the Annunciation and the theatre. There he was constantly visited, it is said, by wild men from the escarpment, Greeks from St Spiridon, Arabs and blacks; he even took to dressing Hav-style, they say, in striped cotton and straw hat.

But then the advantage of going native in Hav is that nobody knows what native is. Now as then, you can take your choice! Chopin, for example, when he came here with George Sand in 1839 after their unhappy holiday in Majorca, chose to live in the Armenian way, rented a house in the Armenian quarter of the Old City and briefly took lessons in Armenian with the city trumpeter of the day. On the other hand James Joyce spent nearly all his time at the Café München, the famous writers' haunt on Bundstrasse, while Richard Burton the explorer, as one might expect, went entirely Arab, strode around the city in burnous and golden dagger, flagrantly snubbed the British Resident, and was rumoured to have got up to terrible things in the darker corners of the Medina – he himself put it around that he had decapitated a man in a bath-house.

Almost the only visiting celebrity not to adopt the ways of the city, in one way or another, was Edward Lear the painter. He set up his studio respectably in a house overlooking the harbour, took on many pupils both English and Havian, and described Hav as 'a very snuffy-uffy, scrumdoochian kind of place'.

There have been many enforced refugees, from many countries and many situations, who have found in this confused and eclectic city a temporary haven. Even as I write, I see one of them on a park bench below. I know him slightly. He is dressed anachronistically even by Hav standards, for he presents an image direct from the

American 1960s: his hair is long and pig-tailed, his moustache is droopy, he wears baseball shoes and patched jeans frayed at the bottom. His guitar is propped against the bench beside him, and he is fast asleep – head back, mouth slightly open, arms on the back of the bench showing (I happen to know) a tattooed dove of peace on one bicep, the words ROLLIN' STONE on the other. He is in his late thirties, I would guess. He is known in Hav as Bob.

Scores of young Americans, evading the draft for the Vietnam war, found their way to Hav in the sixties and seventies, mingling easily enough with the travellers on the hippie route to Afghanistan and Katmandu who used, in those days, sometimes to stop off in the peninsula. As far as I know Bob is the only survivor, having scornfully disregarded the amnesty which took most of the draft evaders home to the United States. He is rumoured to be rich really, and to be supported by subsidies from his family, but I doubt it: he busks with his guitar for money, a familiar figure on the waterfront and the pavements of New Hav, and once he took me to his lodgings, a bed-sitting room in the German quarter plastered all over with anti-war posters, pictures of Joan Baez and Dylan, and touching colour snapshots of his mother and father, gazing into the dark little apartment, with its crumpled bed and chipped mugs by the sink, out of a well-tended garden in Iowa.

Look over there now, through the gateway to the promenade, and you will see, dangling their legs over the edge of the quay, two fugitives of another sort. They are stocky men in their thirties, unshaven rather, in brown baggy trousers and open-necked shirts. Their hair is quite long now, but it was close-cropped when I first saw them, shortly after my arrival in Hav. Unlike Bob, who knows everyone, they are extremely aloof, lodging in a Turkish boarding-house near the central post office, and supporting themselves certainly not by busking, but rumour says by subventions from the British Agency (which is to say, it is knowingly added, the CIA).

They are, we are told, deserters from the Soviet army in Afghanistan, and arrived in Hav nobody knows how – some say by sea. They are supposed to have been thoroughly interrogated by Mr Thorne and his assistants, and then let loose in the city. They seem quite happy. One is a skilled mechanic, and sometimes does odd jobs for people, if he can be made to understand what is needed – very few people speak Russian in Hav now, while the two deserters speak nothing else. The other is variously rumoured to be a fighter pilot and a colonel in the KGB. When I try to speak to them, they smile pleasantly and say nothing: Magda says they would be admirable recruits for the Athenaeum.

Of course they may not be deserters from Afghanistan at all. Another theory is that they are dissident Russian artists, scientists or writers, kept here in reserve, so to speak, until the Western powers feel their propaganda value will be most useful. This has happened before. In the 1950s a distinguished young Russian physicist arrived on a boat from Syria, and immediately made his way to the British Agency. There he stayed for some months safe, sound and secret, awaiting the apposite moment.

But one day a senior British official arrived by train from Ankara supposedly for a last de-briefing of the man, or perhaps a final indoctrination, and thereafter nothing was ever heard of the refugee again. The name of the senior official is lost too: but I wonder, could it have been H.A.R. ('Kim') Philby?

Pace Armand, much the best-known refugee in Hav today is that meditative old Nazi he first pointed out to me – do you remember? – as being very much wanted by the Israelis. The Mossad do not seem to have been searching very hard, for Oberführer Boschendorf is to be found, most days of the week buttonholing people with his story in the pleasure-gardens of the Lazaretto.

I often go there myself, for I love to watch the solemn Hav children enjoying themselves on the biplanes, steamrollers, cocks and wooden camels of the elderly roundabouts, and one afternoon Boschendorf picked on me. 'Please, please, I know you are a writer, I want you to know the truth' – so we went into the old Admiralty House café, and placing his hat carefully on the seat beside him, he told me his tale.

It was perfectly true, he said, as I had doubtless learnt, that during the late war (he always called it the late war) he had been involved in the deaths of Jews, but it was not out of racial hatred. It was because he had cherished since childhood a deep, a truly mystical empathy for the destiny of the Jewish people – 'but am I ever believed in Hav, this snake-pit, this Babylon? Never!' His obsession began when he had been taken as a boy to the Passion Play at Oberammergau. 'The sublime and awful meaning of it! A Jew, the noblest of Jews, condemned to death by his own people – but only, as I realized in revelation that day, as their own imperishable contribution to the destiny of all humanity. It was they themselves that they were sacrificing upon the Cross. Christ was but the image of all his people, the Jews but an enlargement of Christ!'

At first he had seen Hitler and the Nazi party as the embodiment of all evil, the Anti-Christ – 'how I suffered for the Jews with their horrible yellow badges and their degradations'. But then came the war, and he first heard of the Final Solution, the plan to exterminate all the Jews of Europe. 'It was a second revelation to me. The Jews, the Christ-people, were to be sublimated at last in total sacrifice, and join their archetype upon the Cross. I saw it all in ecstasy, those tragic millions, deprived of all but their heritage, in pilgrimage to their own Calvaries. I could not imagine – it would take a Wagner to imagine! – what it would mean for the future of the world, and I came to see Adolf Hitler, as I had long seen Pontius Pilate, as a divine instrument of redemption. I saw all the mighty energies of Germany, beset by enemies on every front, directed to the sacred task – inspired!'

Boschendorf got himself into the SS, and was concerned, as a junior administrative officer, with paperwork for Eichmann's death-trains; but he was never charged with war crimes, and came to Hav after the war not through the tortuous channels of Odessa, but by paying his own fare on the Mediterranean Express. This anti-climax seemed to prey upon his mind.

'They will not listen! They do not hear! Am I a criminal? Am I not rather an agent of God's passion? Was I not to the Jews as Judas was to his master, no more than the means of holy destiny? Have I not risked death to bring them death?' Suddenly unbuttoning his jacket and baring his chest, he showed me tattooed there a Star of David – 'there, as they branded the Jews entering upon their fulfilment so they branded me, at my instructions, Hauptsturmführer, SS, with the badge of the Chosen!'

'Quick, Herr Boschendorf –'

'*Dr* Boschendorf.'

'– quick, button up your shirt, everyone is staring at you.'

'**WHY?**' he shouted. 'Must I be ashamed of my badge?' He rose to his feet and displayed his chest right and left across the café, whose customers were in fact assiduously pretending not to notice. 'MUST I BE ASHAMED?'

One or two of our neighbours now offered me sympathetic smiles, as if to say that they had seen and heard it all before, and the waiters, to a man, conscientiously looked the other way.

'Oh I know what these people' – he threw a hand around the room – 'have been telling you. That's Hav! That's Babylon! They say I am wanted in four continents, don't they? But do I hide myself? Do I hide my badge of sacrament? The Israelis know and respect me for my love of their people, for whom I shed their blood . . .'

I thought he was going to break down. 'I saw you that day with Armand Sauvignon. Did you believe what he told you? Do you know what he did in the late war? He it was, when Jews arrived in Hav, who saw to it that they were shipped to France, and thence to Germany – but he did it not in love, but in hatred. Ask anyone! Oh, we all know Monsieur Sauvignon, novelist, gentleman of France, hypocrite.'

He calmed down presently and politely paid his bill. The head waiter bowed to him respectfully as we left the café. 'I so much enjoyed our talk,' Boschendorf said, 'and feel relieved that you are now in possession of the truth – always a rare commodity in Hav. Use it how you will.' He asked me if I would care to join him on the Electric Ferry back to the Fondaco, but I said no, I would stay on the island a little longer, and watch the children on the merry-go-round as the fairy lights came up.

Who else is sheltering, here in the haven of Hav? A few Israeli deserters, and a few Syrians, who are said to enjoy regular get-togethers at which they damn each others' governments indiscriminately. Plenty of Palestinians, they say. The Caliph's Assyrians. Perhaps one or two of Boschendorf's old comrades. A clutch of Libyans, often to be seen, heads together, gloomily eating kebabs at the Al-Khouri restaurant in the bazaar.

And me, of course, and me. 'What are you running away from?' Magda asked me once. I said I wasn't running away from anything. 'Of course you are,' she said. 'In Hav we are all running.' Perhaps we are, too, each of us finding our own escape in this narrow sultry cul-de-sac. Like many another cage the peninsula of Hav, blazed all about by sun, trapped in dust and moulder, offers its prisoners a special kind of liberation. The harsher, the freer! When the sun goes down on these summer days I feel the city to be less than itself, and look forward impatiently to the hot blast of the morning.

18

Among the Chinese – Feng Shui in Hav – the Palace of Delights – piracy – X's story – ad infinitum

To Yuan Wen Kuo last night, for dinner with M, in the cool of the July evening. We ate early at the Lotus Blossom Garden, and afterwards wandered agreeably around the streets thinking how pleasantly unremarkable everything looked. The Chinese consider it lucky to live in uninteresting times, and it seemed to me that by and large they go to some lengths to live in uninteresting places, too.

Ten miles across the peninsula from the city of Hav proper, which is by any standards unusual, the Chinese have created a town of their own which seems quite deliberately its antithesis: a town without surprises, homogenous in its slatternly makeshift feeling, and imbued with all the standard Chineseness of all the Chinatowns that ever were – the tireless crowds and the smell of cooking, the piles of medicinal roots and powders, the shining varnished dead ducks hanging from their hooks, the burbling bewildered live ones jammed in their market pens, the men in shirtsleeves leaning over the balconies of upstairs restaurants, the severe old ladies on kitchen chairs, the children tied together with string like puppets, as they are taken for walks in parks, the rolls of silk from Shanghai, the bookshops hung with scroll paintings of the Yangtze Gorges, the nasal clanging of radio music, the clic-clac of the abacus, the men playing draughts beneath trees, the disconsolate sniffing dogs, the rich men passing in the back seats of their Mercedes, the poor men pedalling their bicycle rickshaws, the buckets full of verminous threshing fish, the labourers bent double with tea-chests on their backs, the dubious little hotels, their halls brightly lit with unshaded bulbs, the glimpses of girls at sewing-machines in second-storey windows, the fibrous blackened harbour-craft, the old-fashioned bicycles, the shops full of Hong Kong television sets, the Yellow Rose Department Store, the Star Dry-Cleaning Company, the pictures here of Chiang Kai Shek peak-capped against a rising sun, there of Mao Tse-Tung bare-headed against the Great Wall – in short, the threshed, meshed, patternless, hodge-podge, sleepless, diligent and ordinary disorder of the Chinese presence.

How I enjoyed it last night! As we loitered around the streets of Yuan Wen Kuo, digesting our Sautéed Chicken with Wolfberry (recommended to me in Beijing long ago as a specific against depression), I felt extraordinarily reassured by the prosaic activity of it all. I felt in fact, in a calm illogical way, as though I were enjoying a brief spell of home leave from the front.

Perhaps this is what the architects and soothsayers had in mind when, so many centuries ago, they laid out on this inconceivably distant shore the pattern of the first Chinese city west of the Gobi desert. The principles of Feng Shui, the Chinese art of relating buildings to their landscapes, are easy to recognize in Yuan Wen Kuo. Two low hillocks, still bare but for an ornamental tea-house on each of them, stand here half a mile or so from the water's edge, facing south-west. Nothing could be more suitable. Though down the generations the shape of the town has inevitably been blurred, essentially Yuan Wen Kuo still lies, as the Feng Shui men doubtless decreed, between the benevolent arms of the Azure Dragon, the White Tiger, and the Black Tortoise – the three protective ridges which protect it from the north. Halfway up the hill they laid out the main street, for Feng Shui insisted that a site should be commanding, but not exposed; though there are a few rich villas now near the summit of the slope, the bridge itself remains bare to this day, except for the semaphore mast overlooking the fishing harbour at the eastern end.

We are told that the imperial architect Han Tu Chu himself decreed the original ground-plan, but architecturally Yuan Wen Kuo never seems to have been anything special. Perhaps, being so far away, and so vulnerable, the Chinese thought it was hardly worth spending money on expensive buildings there. Marco Polo dismissed it cursorily: 'There is nothing to be said about Yuan Wen Kuo. Let us now move on to other places.' Ibn Batuta thought it 'mean and dirty, with small narrow houses and thieving people', and was glad to get back to the civilized comforts of the Medina, where he was told of a charitable fund established especially to help the victims of extortion in Yuan Wen Kuo. Possibly it was the unimpressive character of the place that encouraged the Chinese authorities, when the time came in the fifteenth century, to build the House of the Chinese Master with such fine extravagance.

By acumen and experience Yuan Wen Kuo survived the Ottoman period – Chinese money from Hav became highly influential in Constantinople – and the town came vigorously into its own again with the arrival of New Hav, which was mostly built by Chinese contractors, and which offered endless opportunities for Chinese speculators. The Palace of Delights (which with its more discreet annexe, the House of Secret Wonders, had existed in Ibn Batuta's time) arose anew as a great pleasure-dome in the middle of Yuan Wen Kuo, and among the Europeans of the concessions became *the* place to go for a racy evening out. As for our own times, they tell me that hardly a development in the Gulf, hardly a new hotel in Abu Dhabi or a university in Oman, fails to send home its quotient of profit to the Chinese financiers of Hav.

The Palace of Delights, by the way, is still there, an ugly concrete block set in a scrubby garden, and is still in its modest way a place of pleasure: there is a restaurant in it, and a concert hall, and there are rival information departments set up by the local factions of Communist China and Taiwan – each with its glass-fronted cabinet full of propaganda booklets, each staffed, as I discovered when I once laboured up the bare concrete steps to their offices, by young men and women with time on their hands to explain their respective points of view until Tuesday week. In its great days, though, the Palace of Delights was something altogether different. I know several people who remember it from the days between the wars, and they make it sound terrific.

There was not just one restaurant then, but a regular covey of them, each serving a different Chinese cuisine, on a different floor, to the music of a different band. Then four or five night clubs pullulated until dawn, and there were fortune-tellers, and beauty parlours, and shops of many kinds, and performing animals, and photographers to take your picture dressed as mandarin or empress, or alternatively not dressed at all. Magicians made rabbits vanish on staircases, fire-eaters stalked the corridors, there were story-tellers, gambling-booths, side-shows offering freaks or dancing-girls or distorting mirrors. You could get married at the Palace of Delights. You could find an amanuensis to write a letter for you, or a wizard to cast you a spell. I have been told that more than a thousand people worked there, and throughout the 1920s and 1930s the profits were immense.

The clientele of the House of Secret Wonders (which has been pointed out to me as a low wooden building, now half-collapsed and covered with tangled creeper) is claimed to have been too distinguished to list – Armand says that in his last years Kolchok himself was a regular customer. The most intriguing rumour I have heard concerns a tall young Englishman with a pale gingery beard, who was said almost to have lived in the place for several months in the years before the First World War. He seemed to be well-off, he had lodgings in a Chinese apartment house along the road, and he apparently had nothing whatever to do with Europeans. After a time he vanished, and people forgot all about him; it is only in recent years that he has been tentatively identified as that queer and beguiling recluse Sir Edmund Backhouse, who lived for most of the rest of his life in Beijing, and deceived the whole world of oriental scholarship with his fake scrolls and fantasies.

I often go to Yuan Wen Kuo. I like to have lunch on the floating restaurant in the harbour, and spend the afternoon sketching from its deck, kept cool with lemonades and thoughtfully adjusted canopies by its obliging owners. I love to watch the fisher-people at work, especially when on festival days they dress up their boats with huge heraldic flags, pennants and trailing crimson dragons, giving them a wonderfully piratical splendour.

Actually, piracy used to be notorious among the Hav Chinese. Fast pirate craft roamed the eastern Mediterranean out of Yuan Wen Kuo, ravaging the Syrian trade routes, preying upon the traffic of the Dardanelles, raiding isolated villages on the coasts of Cyprus and

Lebanon. Even the Venetians, partners in profit to the Hav Chinese, often had occasion to complain about their piracy on the high seas, and in the fifteenth century there were persistent rumours of collusion between the terrible Uskok pirates of the Adriatic and those of Yuan Wen Kuo; a Chinese seaman was among those beheaded after the capture of an Uskok ship by the Venetians in 1458, and to this day in the Yugoslav village of Senj, the old Uskok headquarters, people of faintly oriental cast are said to be descendants of Hav Chinese (though some withered scholars scorn the whole story as merely a semantic confusion between Hav and the Dalmatian island of Hvar . . .).

'I suppose you think,' said M last night, 'that there are no pirates left in Yuan Wen Kuo? You're wrong. I'll introduce you to one right now.' In the twilight we walked up the hill to one of the grand houses at the eastern end of the ridge, immediately below the semaphore, and there we were immediately invited in for coffee by X, as I had better call him, who is one of the Chinese directors of the Casino. This was a very urbane experience, Old Money in the truest sense, since it was originally made out of the silk trade with the Venetians. X is Harvard-educated, his wife was at the Sorbonne, and their house is full of books, pictures Western and Chinese, advanced hi-fi and little Hav terriers. Marvellous vases and ceramic beasts stand about the rooms, and it would not surprise me to learn that some paintings of the Hav-Venetian School are hidden away upstairs. We had our coffee al fresco, looking down over the sea, and it was true X talked in an authentically piratical way about financial coups and deeds of daring – about his success in exploiting the insecurities of Hong Kong, his lucky investments in Singapore during the Japanese occupation, his personal loans to the Castro administration and his profitable stakes in Tanzania. I did not like to ask him if Hitler really had come to Casino Cove, or how well he had known Howard Hughes, but presently M said, 'Go on, tell Jan about Tiananmen.' X, who was otherwise anything but taciturn, at first seemed reluctant, but 'go on,' said Madame X too, 'tell her, where's the harm now? It might be useful, anyway.' And this is what I learnt from Bluebeard's lips.

For years, said X, a group of rich men in Yuan Wen Kuo, calling themselves the Crimson Hand, had supported an active partisan movement against the Communist government in Beijing. They had nothing to do with the Kuomingtang in Taiwan. They were fanatical monarchists, dedicated to the restoration of the Manchu dynasty to the imperial throne of China. Many of the mysterious events reported out of China could be attributed, X said, to them: for example, the supposedly accidental plane crash which in 1971 killed Marshal Lin Biao, Mao's appointed successor. It was rumoured that they had links with the Gang of Four, and that if all had gone well for them the Cultural Revolution would have been climaxed by the deposition of Mao and the restoration of the imperial dynasty to its throne in the Forbidden City.

In 1960 their directors in Hav had conceived a spectacular coup: they decided to abduct the old man who had been, briefly in his childhood, the last emperor of China, then working as a humble clerk in Beijing. They would bring him to Hav as the rallying-point of a great monarchist movement which would, they hoped, sweep all through the world of the overseas Chinese. It would not be a difficult operation, they thought. The Chinese authorities were proud of pointing out Pu Yi, so docile, so well-adjusted to events, as he took the morning bus from his home in the suburbs to his work at a ministry office. Foreigners often saw him, sitting there in his blue work suit, and sometimes spoke to him. His responses were always ideologically correct.

The Crimson Hand's plan was to have a pair of partisans board that morning bus and ride with it until Pu Yi got out at his usual stop at the northern end of Tiananmen Square. He would then be seized in the confusion of the crowd, bundled through the mêlée of the morning commuters into a waiting taxi, and spirited away to Hong Kong and eventually to Hav. Everything was arranged, the get-away taxi, the route to Kwangchow and thence to Hong Kong, where the Crimson Hand had many friends. A dozen dummy runs were tried. Diversions were arranged in Tiananmen Square – a couple of bicyclists were to collide, some subversive leaflets were to be found upon the pavement.

But the very moment they laid hands on Pu Yi as he stepped through the opening door of the bus, they themselves were grabbed by the four harmless-looking passengers stepping out before him, and by two equally innocuous commuters behind their backs. The last of the emperors might be politically cooperative but never for a moment, forty years after his deposition, did the authorities let him out of sight, and the secret policemen of his final bodyguard had not failed him in their duty. The conspirators were quietly executed; Pu Yi continued to take the bus to work until his retirement and peaceful end.

'I hear the Crimson Hand is lying low these days,' said M.

'So I understand,' X replied, 'and yet I have it on very, very good authority that they are grooming their own successor to the throne of the Manchus right here in Hav – rather like [he said to me] your friend the Caliph!'

'Can you imagine?' laughed Madame X, pouring us more coffee.

'*Can you imagine?*' mimicked M, as we walked down the hill again. 'In that house you can imagine anything, can't you? You can imagine X himself as emperor of China!'

But down in the town the Crimson Hand seemed an improbable fancy. It was almost midnight, yet all was as usual among the Hav Chinese: the tireless crowds and the smell of cooking, the piles of roots and powders, the dead ducks and the live ones, the bright bare lights in hotel lobbies, the rickshaws and the limousines, the clic-clac and the threshing fish, and so *ad infinitum* . . .

19

A horrible thing – without religion – Topolino – walking to the hermits – 'on the terrace' – the Cathars – a séance *– Mahmoud disappointed*

A very strange and horrible thing has happened in Hav. Somebody broke into the old Palace chapel and slashed two of the priceless portraits of the Hav-Venetian School which hang inside. The city buzzes with it. The vandals left no explanatory message, but simply daubed a large red tick beside each ruined painting, as though to say that their mission had been accomplished.

Who could have done it? Why? I suggested diffidently to Mahmoud that the motive might have been religious. He dismissed the idea. 'Hav,' he said, 'is not a religious place.'

St Paul would have agreed. There are three references to Hav in his epistles, and none of them are complimentary. Besides complaining about its inhabitants' feckless ineptitude – 'for be not like the people of Hav, who cannot cut wood nor build houses' – he calls them Godless, lustful and not to be trusted. It used to be said that a Pauline epistle to the Havians themselves existed somewhere, in an Anatolian monastery perhaps, or hidden away at Athos: if so, it would make uncomfortable reading for this citizenry.

The Crusaders also found the indigenes of the promontory, by then a mixture of Arabs, Africans, Syrians, Greeks, Turks and Kretevs, spiritually uninspiring. Beycan, in a letter to Raymond of Toulouse, described them as 'worthless and incorrigible', and a contemporary illuminated picture of the castle at Hav shows the inhabitants outside its walls looking horridly gnomish and dog-like. Even the Muslims, it seems to me, have never quite converted this city, though they have been calling it to prayer for nearly a thousand years: the mosques are full enough on Fridays, the Imam of the Grand Mosque is powerful, the presence of the Caliph is never forgotten, but one never feels here the mighty supremacy of the faith, the grand saturation of everyday life, that gives Islam elsewhere in the East its sense of absolute ubiquity. One can hardly imagine a Hav taxi-driver pausing to say his prayers at midday, just as he is unlikely to have dangling at his windscreen an icon of the Virgin Mary or his patron saint – only a plastic model of the Iron Dog, or a little pair of running shoes.

Of course nearly every faith is represented here. There are mosques Sunni and Shia (tucked away in the depths of the Balad). There is a small Buddhist temple at Hen Chaiu Lu, and one sometimes sees its yellow-robed acolytes buying saffron at the morning market. The synagogue is in the old Scuola Levantina of the Venetian Jews; two aged monks are alleged to survive from the Russian monastery of the Holy Ghost, destroyed in the great fire of 1928. The Anglican church may be full of oil-drums, but the Roman Catholics still worship at the French cathedral, the Orthodox Greeks are in Saladin's mosque, the Lutherans still have their chapel next door to the old Residenz, and sundry Maronites, Copts and Nestorians maintain their places of worship, tentative or robust, here and there across the city. The Indian squatters of Little Yalta have built themselves a rickety little Hindu temple by the sea. Once when I was wandering through the Balad in the evening I heard loud enthusiastic singing in an unknown tongue, and walking up an alley to investigate found a happy congregation of black people in full flood of Pentecostal conviction.

But I think it may be true, as Mahmoud said, that Hav as a whole, Hav *in genere* so to speak, is without religion: and as a pagan myself I enjoy this wayward scattering of spirituality, this carefree pragmatism, which makes me feel that I might easily run into those fundamentalists in the Cathedral of St Antoine one day, or find nonagenarian Russian monks helping out with the Buddhist rites.

However I have repeatedly heard of a remarkable deviation from this general rule. Signora Vattani first told me of the hermitage in the eastern moors. She told me that before the war there arrived in Hav from nowhere in particular a strange young Italian nicknamed Topolino, 'Little Mouse' after a small Fiat car popular then.

He dressed himself in a rough brown habit, like a Franciscan, and began giving extempore pavement sermons: and though he was really neither a monk nor a priest – just a layabout, Signora V says – though his political views seemed almost communist and his religious ones inchoate, though he was disgracefully impertinent to the Italian Resident, and for that matter to the late Signor Vattani, besides using terrible language in his homilies, nevertheless he was taken up by some of the Italian families of the concession and established a kind of cult. He lived somewhere in the Balad, but was often to be encountered in his tattered brown cassock at soirées and cocktail parties, and even made an appearance sometimes at palace festivities. For two years running, Signora Vattani says, he took part in the Roof-Race. His favourite preaching-place was the quayside immediately outside the Fondaco, which he used to denounce as a symbol of Italian imperialism.

When the war came, Topolino left the city – to avoid conscription, the Signora maintains – and with a few of his followers built himself a hermitage on the moorland south of Hen Chiau Lu. There he died in 1954, his body being unexpectedly claimed, and taken to Italy, by an eminent Christian Democrat politician ('No, I will not tell you his name – I have my loyalties') who turned out to be the Little Mouse's brother. However I had often been told that his hermitage still existed, and last week I drove out to find it. Nobody could say exactly where it was, but all agreed that you could not take a car all the way. So I started early in the morning, with a packed lunch in a knapsack, and leaving the car at the southern end of China Bay, set off across the tufty grassland into the rolling bare moors, apparently uninhabited, that lie to the south.

It was a marvellous walk. Sometimes the Hav sky seems higher and wider than any sky anywhere, except perhaps in Texas, and on mornings like this the Hav sea, too, seems matchless – so profoundly, bottomlessly blue, so beautifully flecked with the buoys and boats of the Chinese in their wide bay, and falling so lazily, in such long slow waves, upon the silent foreshore. To the south-west silently lay St Spiridon, its church tower protruding over the ridge, and much further away, far out at sea beneath the drifting white clouds, I fancied I could see the distant smudges of other countries altogether – Cyprus? Syria? The Hesperides?

In front the moors looked empty. The magical spring flowers have left Hav now, and the only bright colours in those heathlands were occasional splodges of yellow furze and speckles of a sort of blue poppy they call in Turkish *göz kraliçe*, 'eye of the queen'. Otherwise all was brownish-green, and more brown than green. Sometimes a hawk hovered high above me. Sometimes I started a gamebird from my feet. As the sun came up every rock seemed to flicker with its lizard, and out of the earth the warmth brought a faint aroma, dry, sweet and pungent, which I took to be a memory of all the flowers that had been born, blossomed and died there. But of human life, not a glimpse: looking across the moors suggested to me the battlefields of the Boer war, whose similarly treeless landscapes so often looked just as deserted, until the rifle-fire of the Afrikaners spat and blazed from hidden kopje trenches.

No Mausers, I am glad to say, opened up on me. The morning was absolutely silent. But presently, scrambling around a rocky outcrop (lizards twitching everywhere, dark lichen in declivities), I looked up and saw, on a low rise far ahead, a small patch of tangled green, like an overgrown garden, and beside it, waving, two brown-clad figures. It took me a good hour to get up there; and whenever I looked up again, there those figures always seemed to be, waving their encouragement.

They came the last half-mile or so to meet me, and when I saw them striding easily in my direction I remembered for a moment a Buddhist mystic I encountered thirty years ago in the Himalayas, who seemed hardly to walk at all over the snows, but rather to levitate. However these ascetics of Hav turned out to be anything but ethereal – light on their feet perhaps, because they were very thin, but smiling very straightforward smiles, offering me jolly greetings in Italian, and showing evidence all too clear, in their stooped old figures and arthritic-looking fingers, that they were as corporeal as anyone else. Their cassocks, tied with straw ropes in monkly style, were neatly patched. They wore rubber flip-flops, incongruously blue and yellow, upon their feet. They had straggly grey beards, and both looked to me in their seventies.

I was ashamed to find myself breathless as these old men, so agile despite their infirmities, cheerfully paced me over the moor. But they laughed my apologies aside. It was no competition, they said, since they lived such wonderfully healthy lives out there; and indeed when we reached the hermitage, and the seven other members of the community, four men, three women, crowded around to welcome me, they did look extraordinarily spry, though all were of a similar age, and gave the impression that were it not for the deep tans of so many summers on the moorland, their cheeks might have been quite rosy.

They seemed to inhabit a pergola: at least the wide shelf of the rising ground there, perhaps a hundred yards long, had been roofed with a construction of wood and wire which, covered as it was all over with wild vines, meant that the place was half indoors, and half out. It was all green and leafy, wonderfully cool and it was bisected by a small stream which came out of a conduit above, and went splashing away through the heather towards the sea. Along this dappled belvedere were eight or nine little wooden huts, very well built of rough oak, which formed the cells of the community, together with a store-house at the end. Outside was a long trestle table with benches, and an iron stove whose chimney disappeared through the leaves of the pergola. The hermits produced water in thick white china mugs, and we all sat down at the table while they explained things.

What did they call themselves? I asked. Nothing. What were their beliefs? Nothing: they were a community of agnostics, dedicated to the certainty of uncertainty. Would they describe themselves as disciples of Topolino? No, they had simply been friends of his, who had all chosen the same course of life. How did they live? 'We have our garden, we used to do some fishing, and fortunately some of us have a little money of our own.' Four of them, they said, smiling affectionately at one another, were married couples. One of the men was a widower, whose wife had lived with him 'on the terrace', as they described their situation. The others were bachelors. 'And we are all friends,' they cried triumphantly, 'after forty-five years on the terrace!'

Forty-five years! 'Come with me,' said one of the old women, scrambling off the bench and taking me by the hand. She led me into her cabin, which was bare, and neat, and had two beds and a vase of eye-of-the-queen on the table. 'There we all are,' she said; on the wall, a little mildewed, was a photograph of a dozen laughing young men and women, wearing summer clothes but holding in front of them, each one, a cassock and a cord. '12 April, 1940,' said my companion, 'the day we took our vows – and there's Topolino in the middle.' He looked a splendid fellow, the very opposite of a little mouse, being tall, muscular and evidently exuberant. He alone was wearing his cassock already, beneath a wide Hav hat, and he was holding a paper of some kind scrunched above his head with one hand, while with the other he waved to the camera in a gesture of delight. In the background I could see the walls of the Fondaco, and at each end of the picture two or three small boys, in short trousers, were peering mischievously around the edges of the group.

'Where are you?' I asked my companion. She showed me herself in the front row, wearing a Spanish-looking blouse with full frilled sleeves, and white trousers. 'Oh,' she said, 'I was very modern then.'

I ate my picnic lunch with them, on the trestle table, in the vine-patterned shade. They ate salads and what looked like cold noodles. I offered them some of my wine, but they said no, they hadn't touched the stuff for forty years – 'but we drank it often enough before!' They were all educated people, two of them at least speaking excellent English, and several of them French. They were Italian by birth, they told me, but now regarded themselves as being of no nationality. 'We are the people of nowhere.' Nihilists? Certainly not, for they believed that nothing and everything were the same thing. They had long outgrown any instinct for material possession, they said, but at the same time they had foresworn from the very start any striving for mystic enlightenment. They never prayed or meditated, or even read much any more. If they worshipped anything, it was life itself; if they had any doctrine, it could best be identified as a sense of humour.

Of course, said I, they had advantages over other varieties of eremite, in that they were people of intellectual resource, were evidently not destitute, and seemed to have no responsibilities towards anyone else on earth. It was true, they readily admitted. They were mostly the children of business and official families of the Italian concession, and some of them had inherited properties in

Italy, which had relieved them of many worries – occasionally for instance some of their members had gone to Beirut, or even to Italy, for medical or dental treatment. Also they often bought food in Yuan Wen Kuo, all walking there and back together – 'we enjoy the exercise'. I said they must seem exotic figures, the nine of them, strolling down the main street past the Palace of Delights. 'Oh do you think so?' they said.

They seemed to me on the whole the happiest, the friendliest, the most truly banal and the most entirely selfish people I had met in all Hav. They seemed drained of everything but satisfaction. All nine walked back with me to the start of the outcrop, and all shook my hand affectionately. I said they had been described to me as the only religious people in Hav, and this made them laugh. 'No,' said one of the old men in an uncharacteristically ironic tone of voice, 'the only religious people in Hav are the Cathars.'

And so I first heard of the Cathars of Hav. I thought it odd that nobody had mentioned them before, and when I asked about them people seemed evasive. The Cathars were somewhat like Freemasons, I heard it suggested. They no longer existed, somebody else said, or if they did, were all immensely old. Magda just laughed, when I asked her. Dr Borge looked knowing.

I learned something of their beginnings from Jean Antoine's *Hav et les Crusades*, which was published in 1893, but is still the only work on the subject. The Cathar heresy of France, it appears, probably originated among the knights of the First Crusade. They had picked up its basic ideas from the Manicheans, whose roots were in Babylonia, and whose religion was based upon the existence of two equal principles in the world, the Good and the Evil, the Light and the Dark, both to be placated. The Yezidis of modern Iraq, who seem to have had Manichean origins, have come over the centuries to place far more emphasis on the Evil One than on the Good, and have been seen by foreigners as Satan-worshippers – they will not pronounce the sound *sh*, because Satan abhors it, they will not wear the colour blue, because Satan does not like it, they will not eat lettuce because Satan is associated with it, having once hidden under its leaves in time of emergency.

The Crusaders on the other hand evolved their ideas into a

recognizably Christian heresy. Like Pelagianism, it postulated that Man was essentially the master of his own destiny – human will was far more important than divine decree; and it was supposed too that Satan had never fallen from heaven, but was still co-regnant with God, dividing the responsibilities of omnipotence, each pulling mankind towards opposite poles of morality. In France Catharism in a more sophisticated form so gripped the imagination of people in the south-east, particularly, that the thirteenth century Albigensian Crusade was required to exterminate it, the last of the cultists holding out to the bitter end in the hilltop fortresses of Roussillon and Languedoc.

According to Antoine, Hav was a stronghold of Catharism among the Crusaders. Among their Armenian followers were several Paulicians, who held similar views to the Manicheans, and are said powerfully to have influenced the knights – Katourian the minstrel was one. Beynac, himself a native of Roussillon, is said to have been an early convert, and many of his lieutenants followed suit. More than that, they and the Armenians converted to their beliefs many of Hav's cosmopolitan citizens, Greek, Arab, Turkish, Syrian, so that when in 1191 Saladin put an end to Christian rule in the peninsula, and the Crusaders surrendered the castle to the sound of Katourian's lament, they left behind them under Arab rule a resolute Cathar cult of a unique kind. 'Of all the legacies that remain to us of the Crusader era in Hav,' wrote Antoine in 1893, 'the most mysterious and perhaps the most resilient is the movement of Cathars, which has its connections throughout the Near East, and which long ago crossed the borders of sect or confessional, to become a fraternity still influential – 700 years later – within the body politic of the city.'

It was Fatima Yeğen who led me to the modern Cathars. Yes, she told me cautiously when I mentioned the movement, she knew of their existence, but their affairs were very secret. 'You cannot guess how secret, how private.' However she would do her best to help, and a few days later, when I was eating my picnic lunch in the Serai garden, she accosted me theatrically. 'You know the subject we were discussing – those people, you know? Come tonight to the hotel, nine o'clock, and you shall meet somebody who will tell you about them' – and conspiratorially, looking right and left, she flitted away among the flower-beds. 'Nine o'clock sharp,' she said over her shoulder.

So that night I turned up at the hotel, where Fatima was waiting for me expectantly, nervously I thought, inside her kiosk. 'Now you must remember,' she said, 'that I have sworn you to secrecy – you must not let me down.' Never, I assured her, and she stopped outside one of the downstairs bedroom doors, said, 'In there', and left me. I entered, and two young men rose to greet me. One was Yasar Yeğen, who had driven me down the Staircase on my very first day in Hav. The other, introduced to me simply as George, was the man who had spat at me outside the Palace, when the gendarme dismounted and beat him up.

Neither mentioned our previous encounters. They shook my hand gravely, offered me Cyprus brandy from a bottle that stood, with a couple of toothmugs, on the bedside table, and said they were ready to take me to a Cathar meeting that evening.

'You must realize,' said Yasar, 'that we do this only because we have heard good things of you, and we may want you to give evidence.'

'Evidence?' I did not like the sound of that.

'We want you to tell the world, if it is necessary, that you saw the Cathars of Hav this very night in *séance*.'

He was using the word, I knew, in its French sense, but all the same it gave me an eerie jolt.

'*If it is necessary*, I say. You will know. Otherwise you must swear to me that you will reveal nothing – where you have been, who you saw. You must ask me no questions – promise me.'

'I promise.'

'Very well, then we need not blindfold you. Try not to look where we are going.'

I tried hard, and it was not difficult. We rode in George's Citroën, Yasar in the back with me, and I could scarcely help observing that we sped straight across Pendeh Square, turned behind the old legation buildings, and entered the Medina by the small gateway, only just wide enough for a car, which is called Bab el Kelb, 'Dog's Gate'. After that I was lost. We went up this alley and that, more than once seemed to double back on our tracks, crossed a square or two, passed through one of the open bazaars; and finally, leaving

George and the car in a yard full of iron pipes and asbestos sheeting, and half used as a football pitch, Yasar and I entered the back door of one of the towering old Arab houses which form the core of the Old City. I could see the minaret of the Grand Mosque over a rooftop to my right, but for the life of me I could not tell which side of it was facing us. Their secret was safe. I had no idea where I was.

Up some steep stairs we went, across a landing, around an open gallery above the interior courtyard of the house, up some more stairs, through what appeared to be some kind of robing room, for there were outdoor clothes on hooks, hangers and chairs all over it, until we entered a small chamber, more a cupboard than a room, through whose wall I could hear a muffled drone of voices, sometimes a single speaker, sometimes a chorus, talking what sounded like French. Yasar closed the door. We were in utter darkness. He pulled aside a curtain then, and through a glazed and grilled little window I could see into a dimly lit room below.

'The *séance*,' whispered Yasar. 'You see the Cathars of Hav.'

Actually, now that I was there it reminded me more of a Welsh eisteddfod than a spiritualist meeting, for the forty or fifty people down there were all strangely robed. On the left sat the women, in white, veiled like nuns. On the right were the men, in black, with cowls worn far forward over their faces. And on a dais in the middle sat a dozen men whose robes were bright red, whose turbans were wound around the lower halves of their faces like Tuaregs, and whose tall wooden staves were each capped with the shining silver figure of an animal, tail extended. I could not hear what was being said. It seemed to be a sort of ritualized conference, for sometimes one of the elders spoke alone, sometimes a man or woman rose from the floor to make a contribution, and sometimes the whole company broke into the droning mechanical chant that I had heard before.

'Remember,' said Yasar, 'you know nobody here.'

I nodded, but wondered. Were not some of those veiled figures familiar to me, beneath their theatrical cloaks and hoods, behind their veils? Did not that woman in the front row, the tensely crouching one at the end – did she not look a little like – who was it? – Yes! Anna Novochka's misanthropist housekeeper? Was it possible – surely not – but was it possible that the man speaking now, his hood deeply down over his forehead, was standing somewhat in

Missakian's stance? Could they conceivably be Assyrians, those stocky men just behind him? Was it altogether fancy, or could I detect above the red veil of the most stalwart of the elders the tunnel pilot's lordly stare?

I could be sure of none of them. I was disturbed and bewildered, and began to see the most unlikely people disguised in those queer vestments among the shadows of the chamber – the Caliph, Mr Thorne, Chimoun, even crazed old Dr Boschendorf! They were probably all in my imagination, and I did not have long to search for more substantial clues, because at a word from the chief elder, and a knock on the floor from his stave, the company rose to its feet and turned towards the dais, as if they were about to recite a creed or mantra. Instantly Yasar drew the curtain and hurried me out of the room, down the stairs and into the car where George was waiting.

'You must ask us no questions,' said Yasar. 'You have the evidence, if it is needed. Remember your promise.'

'*Remember*,' said George, less kindly I thought.

'Yes, yes, I remember. But just let me ask you one thing – only one, and nothing more I swear. Who were the men on the platform, the ones in red? Were they priests?'

The young men looked at each other, and shrugged. 'I don't know how you say it in English,' said Yasar, 'but we call them *Les Parfaits*.'

The Perfects!

Not Prefects – Perfects!

I told nobody about my visit to the upper room of the Cathars, but I did tell Mahmoud that I had been to see the hermits, and that they only confirmed what he had said about Hav – they were not in the least religious. He was intensely disappointed. He had thought them the great exceptions. As a matter of fact in his adolescence he had cherished the ambition of joining them one day in a life of prayer and meditation. 'They were my ideal,' he said.

'Why *didn't* you join them, then?'

'Why was I never a roof-runner? Cowardice, Jan, pure cowardice. I have lived a life of it.' Having met Topolino's followers for myself, I did not think much courage was needed to join them on the terrace: but I was not so sure about the Cathars.

20

A visit to the troglodytes

All this time (it may have crossed your mind) and I still had not clambered the escarpment to the cave-homes of the Kretevs, the most compelling of all the Havians! I wonder why? Sometimes I was afraid of disillusionment, I suppose, in this city of reappraisals. Sometimes I reasoned that I should end with the beginning, and keep those atavists for my last letter. And sometimes I felt that, what with the Cathars, and the British Agency's radio masts, and the peculiar island Greeks, I was surfeited with enigma. But I kept in touch with Brack, and at the market the other day he beckoned me over to his stall. He said that if I wanted to come to Palast (which is, so far as I can make out, more or less what the troglodytes themselves call their village) I had better come that very day – if I brought my car I could join the market convoy when it went home in the afternoon. Trouble was brewing in Hav, he said, bad trouble, and it might be my only chance. He shook his head in a sorrowful way, and his ear-rings glinted among his dreadlocks. So at three o'clock – sharp! – I drove down to the truck park, and found the Kretev pick-ups all ready to go. Brack leant from his cab and gestured me to follow him. The other drivers, starting up their engines, stared at me blankly.

Trouble? All seemed peaceful, as we drove along the edge of the Balad and into the salt-flats. The old slave settlement looked just as listless as it had when I first saw it, so dim-lit and arid, through the windows of the Mediterranean Express. Some small boys were playing football on the waste ground beside the windmills. Away to the west I thought I could distinguish Anna's villa, in the flank of the hills, and imagined her settling down, now as always, to tea, petits fours and her current novel (she is very fond of thrillers). The usual lonely figures were labouring in the white waste of the salt-pans, and now and then one of the big salt-trucks rumbled by on its way to the docks.

But just as we left the marshes and approached the first rise of the escarpment, Brack leant out of his window again and pointed to something in the sky behind us: and there were two black aircraft, flying very low and very fast out of the sea – except for the passing airliners, the first I had ever seen over Hav.

In the event I did not have to clamber to the caves, for one can drive all the way. It is a rough, steep and awkward track though, and most of the Kretevs left their trucks at a parking place at the foot of the escarpment, piling vigorously into the back of Brack's pick-up and into my Renault. Thus I found myself squeezed tight in my seat by troglodytes when I drove at last into the shaly centre of Palast – which, like so many things in Hav, was not as I expected it to be.

I had supposed it something like the well-known cave settlements of Cappadocia, whose people inhabit queer white cones of rock protruding from the volcanic surface. But Palast is much more like the gypsy colony of Sacramonte in Spain, or perhaps those eerie towns of cave-tombs that one finds in Sicily, which is to say that it is a township of rock-dwellings strung out on both sides of a cleft in the face of the escarpment. Wherever I looked I could see them, some in clusters of five or six, some all alone, some at ground level, some approached by steps in the rock, or ladders, some apparently altogether inaccessible high in the cliff face. Many had tubs of greenery outside, or flags of bright colours, and some had white-washed surrounds to their entrances, like picture frames.

The flat floor of the ravine was evidently common ground, with a row of wells in the middle. Shambled cars, not unlike my own, were parked at random around it, stocky ponies wandered apparently at liberty, hens scooted away from my wheels. Out of some of the cave doors, which were mostly screened with red and yellow bead curtains, heads poked to see us come – a woman with a pan in her hand, an old man smoking a cigar, half a dozen boys and girls who, spotting my unfamiliar vehicle, came tumbling out to meet us. Soon I was sitting at a scrubbed table in Brack's own ground-floor cave, drinking hot sweet tea with his young wife, whose name sounded like Tiya, and being introduced to an apparently numberless stream of neighbours, of all ages, who came pressing into the cave.

When I say I was being introduced, it was generally in a kind of dumb show. Some of the men spoke Turkish, some a little Arab or French, but the women spoke only Kretev. We shook hands solemnly, exchanged names and inspected each others' clothes. Here I was at a disadvantage. I was wearing jeans, a tennis shirt and my yellow Australian hat, rather less spring-like now after so much bleaching by the suns of Hav. They on the other hand were distinctly not wearing the jumbled neo-European hand-downs I had expected from the appearance of their market men on the job; on the contrary, they were in vivid reds and yellows, like the door curtains, the women in fine flowing gypsy skirts, the men in blazing shirts over which their long tangled hair fell to great effect. They jammed the table all around me and I felt their keen unsmiling eyes concentrated hard, analysing my every gesture, my every response. Their faces were very brown, and they smelled of a musky scent. Sometimes their ear-rings and bangles tinkled. Whenever I was not talking they fell into a hushed but animated conversation among themselves.

'They want to know,' Brack told me, 'what you think of our caves.' The caves seemed fine to me, if his own was anything to go by. It was far more than a cave really, being four or five whitewashed rooms, three with windows opening on to the common ground outside, furnished in a high-flown romantic mode, tapestry chair-covers and mahogany sideboards, and lit by electric lights beneath flowered glass lampshades definitely not designed by Peter Behrens of AEG. Everything was brilliantly clean: it all reminded me of a Welsh farmhouse, not least the miscellaneous mementoes of Brack's naval service that were neatly displayed in the glass-fronted corner cupboard. The water, I was told, had to be drawn from the wells, but the electricity came from the Kretev's own generator.

It all seemed fine, I said. But was there any truth in the rumour that the caves really joined together, forming a secret labyrinth inside the escarpment? They did not, as I expected, laugh at this. They talked quite earnestly among themselves before Brack interpreted.

'We don't think so,' he said, 'we have never found one, but our people have always maintained that there is one great tunnel in the mountain behind us, and they say a great leader of our people long ago sleeps in there, and if we are ever in danger he will awake from sleep with his warriors and come out to help us. That is the story.' What about the treasures of the old Kretevs, the goblets, the golden horses, which I had been told from time to time were picked up on the escarpment? Then they *did* laugh. No such luck, they said, and when many years before some archaeologists had excavated the barrow-tombs down in the salt-flats, which were said to be the graves of primeval Kretevs, they found nothing inside but old bits of natural rock, placed there, it was supposed, because they bore some resemblance to human faces.

There was a thumping noise outside, and a rumble, and with a flicker the lights came on. Then we had supper. Everyone stayed for it, even the children who had been hanging about their parents' legs or staring at me from the doorway. It was goat stew in a huge tureen, with fibrous bread that Tiya had made. We helped ourselves with a wooden spoon and ate out of a variety of china bowls, some brought in from neighbouring caves because there were too few to go round. We never stopped talking. We talked about the origins of the Kretevs ('we came out of the earth, with horses'). We talked about the snow raspberries (not so plentiful as they used to be, but then that made for higher prices). We talked about Kretev art ('they do not understand your question') and Kretev religion ('we do not talk about that'). We talked about earning a living (their goat-herds, their market-gardens, their grassland where the cattle grazed). We talked about their language, but inconclusively; every now and then I heard words which seemed vaguely familiar to me, but when I asked their meaning no bells were rung, and when I invited the Kretevs to count up to ten for me, hoping to recognize some Celtic affinities, I recognized not a single numeral. What were their names again? Around the room we went, but not a name seemed anything but totally alien – Projo (I write as I heard them), Daraj, Stilts, what sounded improbably like Hammerhead. They had no surnames, they said: just the one name each, that was all. They needed no more. They were Kretevs!

Not Havians, I laughed, and that brought us to the condition of the city which lay, feeling a thousand miles away, through the string-bead curtains of that cave, and down the gulley across the salt-flats. What was happening down there? What was the vague feeling of malaise or conspiracy that seemed to be gathering like a cloud over the city? Who slashed the paintings in the palace chapel? Most ominously of all, what were those black aircraft we had seen on the way up? None of them knew. 'Bad things,' said Brack, 'that's all we know.' Were they worried? They did not seem to be. 'We are here, it is there.' Besides, they had no high opinion of life down on the peninsula. 'Do you not know,' said Brack, speaking for himself now, 'what sort of people they are? Each talks behind the other. Have you not discovered? Hav is never how it says. So . . .' He splayed his hands in a gesture of indifference, and all around the table the brown faces gravely nodded, or leaned backwards with a sigh. 'We are here, it is there.'

And did they, I asked, ever see a Hav bear these days? Supper was over by then, and we were drinking out of a cheerful assortment of tumblers, cups and souvenir mugs from Port Said the Kretevs' own liqueur, made from the little purple bilberries which abound on the upper slopes of the escarpment, and alleged to cause hallucinations, like the magic mushroom, if you drink too much of it. There was silence for a moment. Somebody made a joke and raised a laugh. They talked among themselves in undertones. Then, 'Come on,' said Brack, taking a torch from the mantelpiece, 'come with us.' Out we trooped into the moonlit night, the whole company of us, some people scattering to their own caves to pick up torches; and so in an easy straggle, fifteen or twenty of us I suppose, torch beams wavering everywhere up the ravine, we walked up the gravel track towards the face of the escarpment. Above us the rocks rose grey and blank; all around the lights of the cave-dwellers twinkled; low in the sky, across the flatlands, a half-moon was rising. Through some of the open cave-doors I could see the flickering screens of TV sets, and discordant snatches of music reached us stereophonically from all sides. The engine of the generator rhythmically thumped.

It was a stiff climb that Brack led us in the darkness, off the sloping floor of the ravine, up a winding goat path, very steep, which took us high up the escarpment bluff, until those lights of Palast were far below us, the music had faded, and only the beat of the generator still sounded. The Kretevs, though considerably more out of breath than the hermits of the eastern hills, were not dismayed. They were full of bilberry juice, like me. The women merrily hitched up their skirts, the men flashed their torches here and there, they laughed and chatted all the way. They seemed in their element, in the dark, on the mountain face, out there in the terrain of *Ursus hav* and the snow raspberries.

Quite suddenly, almost as though it had been switched off, we could no longer hear the noise of the generator. 'When we hear the silence,' said Brack, 'we know we are there' – for at the very same moment we crossed a small rock ridge and found ourselves in a dark gulley, with a big cave mouth at the end of it. The Kretevs stopped their chatter and turned their torches off. 'We must be quiet now,' whispered Brack. In silence we walked up the gulley, and I became aware as we neared the cave of a strange smell: a thick, warm, furry, licked smell, with a touch of that muskiness that I had noticed on the Kretevs themselves – an enormously old smell, I thought, which seemed to come from the very heart of the mountain itself.

We entered the cave in a shuffling gaggle, like pilgrims, guided only by Brack's torch. It was not at all damp in there. On the contrary, it felt quite particularly dry, like a hayloft, and there was no shine of vapour on its walls, or chill in its air. The further we went, the stronger that smell became, and the quieter grew the Kretevs, until they walked so silently, on tip-toe it seemed, that all I could hear was their breathing in the darkness. Nobody spoke. Brack's torch shone steadily ahead of us. The passage became narrower and lower, so that we had to bend almost double to get through, and then opened out once more into what appeared to be a very large low chamber, its atmosphere almost opaque, it seemed to me, with that warmth and must and furriness. Brack shone his torch around the chamber: and there were the bears.

At first (though by now I knew of course what to expect) I did not realize they were bears. They looked just like piles of old rugs, heaped on top of one another, like the discarded stock of a carpet-seller. They lay in heaps around the walls of the chamber, motionless. But the Kretevs began to make a noise then, a sort of soothing carressing noise, something between singing and sighing, and all around the cave I heard a stirring and a rustling – grunts, pants, heavings. When Brack shone his torch around again, everywhere I could see big brown heads raised from those huddles, and bright green eyes staring back at us out of the shadows. The bears were not in the least hostile, or frightened. One or two rolled their heads over sleepily, like cats, burying them in their paws. One was caught by the torch-light in the middle of a yawn. None bothered to get to their feet, and as the Kretevs ended their crooning and we stole away down the passage again, bumping into one another awkwardly in the silence, I could hear those animals settling down to sleep again in their soft and fusty privacy.

When we reached the open air again the moon was glistening upon the salt-flats below, and the Kretevs burst once more into laughter and conversation. They seemed refreshed and reassured by their visit to the bears, and gave me the impression that they would one and all sleep like logs that night, in their own scattered caverns of the hillside.

I did too, in my sleeping-bag in the cool back room of Tiya's cave, and got up in the morning in time to say goodbye to the market men before the dawn broke. The goat-herds and gardeners were already climbing up the ravine. 'Come back again,' said Brack as he shook my hand, but I felt I never would. 'Look after yourselves,' I said in return. When I left Palast myself, a couple of hours later, all the young men had gone, and there were only women, children and old men to see me off. Their farewell was rather formal. They stood there still and silent, even the children, as I turned on the engine and started the Renault's reluctant ignition (not what it was when the tunnel pilots had it). 'Goodbye,' I said, 'goodbye.' They smiled their wistful smiles, and raised their hands uncertainly.

AUGUST

21

The Agent writes – symptoms – trouble – a decision in the night – saying goodbye – looking back

When I got home from my visit to the Kretevs Signora Vattani knocked on my door with a letter for me. It looked vaguely official, and important, or she would have left it on the table downstairs. She doubtless thought it was a social invitation, but it wasn't.

My dear Miss Morris [it said],
I am not certain whether in fact you consider yourself a British subject, but I think it best to let you know that according to our information the internal difficulties of Hav will shortly be coming to a head, and I consider it my duty to advise you to leave the city as soon as is convenient. You will I am sure be able to make your own arrangements.
My wife sends you her regards.

> Yours sincerely,
> Ronald Thorne
> British Agent

I immediately went round to the Aliens Office and presented the letter to Mahmoud. What did it mean? Nothing, he said, nothing. It was just rumours, that was all. I should take no notice of it. What could the British Agent know that he didn't know? – why, he had been with the Governor himself that very morning. 'But if I were you,' Mahmoud added, 'I would not show the letter to anyone else.'

I showed it to everyone, of course, but they nearly all pooh-poohed it, or professed to. As the days passed, nevertheless, I felt the city's usual indeterminate disquiet, its habitual grumble or frisson in the air, unmistakably resolving itself into something more menacing. If I had been haunted before by the Iron Dog or the Cathars, I was pursued now by the implication of those two black aircraft.

Yes, what about those aircraft? Few people admitted to having seen them at all, but those who did said they were probably just passing over, or taking part in Turkish war games. Then it seemed to me that there were rather more of those baffling tramp steamers coming and going in the harbour, vague of destination and improbable of cargo, but Chimoun assured me that it was 'merely a seasonal fluctuation of traffic'. The gunboat moored at the Lazaretto had steam up one morning, for the first time since I have been in Hav, and that afternoon I found the Fondaco wharf screened off by canvas awnings, and was told to go round the back way by a sentry shouting down at me from the roof; I peered through a gap when he wasn't looking, but all I could see was a pile of banana boxes. The annual football match between the Salt Men and the Runners, representing in effect the Balad and the Medina, was indefinitely postponed 'owing to probable weather conditions', and it was announced in the *Gazette* that in future the Electric Ferry services would end at sunset, instead of midnight as before.

Little symptoms, symptoms in the mind perhaps. Nobody seemed to be worrying. Signora Vattani said: 'Believe me, I know what trouble is. I've seen enough of it in my time. I know when trouble's in the air.' Armand said: 'Yes, *ma chérie*, these are feelings that we all have after our first few months in Hav. It is like an island here. After a few months we pine to get off – then we pine to get back again.' Magda said darkly: 'You're right, you're right, at last you feel it, you are becoming the true Havian at last.' Fatima Yeğen said she did not like to think about such things. I took to listening to the BBC news each night, but there was no mention of Hav.

I telephoned Ronald Thorne and asked him if he would elucidate his warning, or allow me to come to the Agency to talk about it. 'Really, Miss Morris,' he said, 'I think I have done my duty in writing to you. These are busy times for me. You must take your own counsel on these matters.' I telephoned Hav 001, too, but it was always engaged. I kept my eye on the various refugees I knew in the city, the Israelis, the Libyans, those two Russians, somehow supposing that they would be more sensitive than the rest of us to stirrings in the political atmosphere: they were still drinking in the same cafés, loitering around Pendeh Square, sitting on the waterfront, as they always did.

But by last week nobody could ignore the signs. On the Monday morning, very early, there was an explosion somewhere, and the electric power was off all day. The *Gazette* appeared with half its front page blank, and worshippers going to the Grand Mosque for morning prayers found that indecipherable graffiti in red paint had been scrawled all over its arcades. On Wednesday I was told there had been some kind of riot in the Balad, and when I walked across the square I found the palace guards no longer in their white drill and epaulettes, with those quaint guns and those stylized smiles: they were in camouflage suits now, held automatic rifles, and seemed to be cultivating the facial expressions of martial art. 'Don't worry,' Mahmoud said, 'don't worry, that always happens at the end of July – this is their training time.' But when I drove south from the Medina later that day, intending to draw some pictures of the Iron Dog, the track was blocked with barricades, and notices said that the Conveyor Bridge was closed to traffic for essential repairs.

Now everybody was beginning to be anxious, without admitting it, without knowing why. The *Gazette* told us nothing, but nobody could fail to see the two black aircraft when they came back on Thursday morning, because they flew deafeningly backwards and forwards very low over the centre of the city, shaking the windows with the thunderous blast of their engines. There was a long, long line at the bank when I went to collect my draft. Fatima reported an unusual number of passengers leaving on the train. Somebody said they had seen all the rich yachts from Casino Cove sailing away together, as in convoy, south past St Spiridon towards Cyprus. At the café in Pendeh Square I met a disconsolate group of young Germans who had come to Hav on an overland adventure tour: they had expected to stay a week, they said, but had been ordered back up the Staircase that same night. When I asked Armand what could be happening, he said testily: 'How can I know? I am just an old pensioner. I am no longer in touch.'

On Thursday night, soon after midnight, I heard a single

protracted burst of automatic gunfire, somewhere quite close. Nothing more. I ran to my balcony and looked out across the city, but all seemed peaceful. A few people were walking along the pavement below. The last No. 2 tram was disappearing under the Brandenburg. I could see the lights of a ship moving slowly down the harbour past the dim outline of the Lazaretto. The Serai domes shone luminously above the roofs, and made me think of Diaghilev, the King of Montenegro, and Rimsky-Korsakov playing his piano in the palace garden. High above us I could sense, rather than see, the grey shape of the castle, up whose winding path, in a few hours, Missakian would be labouring with his trumpet for another day's lament – how many had the city heard, I wondered, and with what variety of feeling, since the Crusaders marched off between the silent ranks of Arabs to their waiting galleys at the quay?

I was moved by the moment, and by the thought of all the life and history, all the secrets and confusions, all the truths and fantasies, all the strains of blood and conflict that surrounded me there that night. I felt it was all mine! But though I heard no more gunfire, and though as the time passed, while I stood watching in the warm night, a profound and peaceful silence fell upon the city, yet I decided there and then to take the Agent's advice and make my arrangements to leave.

The city was frightened now. In the bazaar a myriad rumours were going about – of a coup d'état caught in the bud, of an impending Turkish takeover, a Palestinian conspiracy, a Greek plot, a kidnapping of the Caliphate or an assassination attempt at the Palace . . . Mahmoud denied them all, but was increasingly evasive. Remarkably few people, I noticed, were taking their lunches at the Athenaeum. Another note arrived for me, this time from Mario Biancheri: 'I shall not be at the market tomorrow. I have to go to Istanbul. I shall be at the Pera Palas. Ciao.'

When I went to the station to buy my ticket out, they told me that from that night the train would come no further than the old frontier. 'I can sell you a ticket, but you will have to make your own way up the Staircase – no rebates.' I decided to drive up there and abandon the car at the station, or give it to Yasar, if he was around. I spent the morning saying my goodbyes, but already it seemed Hav's brittle society was coming apart.

Fatima, for instance, the first of my friends in the city, was not expected at the hotel that day, or the next either – they were not sure when she would be back, in fact. Armand was not at his apartment, nor at the Bristol, where the barman told me he had not been in for his noontime Pernod for a couple of days. I looked in at the Fondaco café, but Chimoun was not at his soup, and the two Russians were nowhere to be seen along the promenade. I had a last lunch at the Athenaeum with Dr Borge ('you see, you see!') and Magda ('remember the Victor's Party?') but Mahmoud was nowhere to be found – 'he's probably with the Governor,' his assistant said.

I rang the Caliph again, and this time I got him. I congratulated him on not having been kidnapped. 'The Wazir will miss you,' he said. I found Bob on the quay strumming his guitar as usual to a little thing of his own:

> *Nothin's goin' to be the same, no, no,*
> *Not while the years keep comin'.*

He grasped my upper arm, looked me straight in the eye and said: 'The first rule of life: you never know, you never know.' The Signora was predictably tearful, as she accepted two months' rent in lieu of notice, and gave me a picture of herself, in slimmer times, to remember her by. When I threw my bags into the front of the car old Abdu, the Egyptian from the Ristorante Milano downstairs, came running out of his door to wish me luck – 'but you will be back – you know the saying, "He who has drunk the water of Hav . . .!" ' I gave the thumbs up to the Circassian sentries when I drove for the last time around the square, and for all their camouflage gear they responded with their old parade-ground smiles. Just as I rounded the castle ridge, to take the road north through the Balad, with a howl those black planes hurled themselves again out of the eastern hills.

Above me on the Staircase a long line of cars was already climbing. Others were following me across the flats. The winding track itself did not seem half so thrilling as it had when Yasar raced me down it five months before, and I drove up easily enough in the lingering dust haze raised by the cars ahead. Halfway up a Kretev stood, with his flock of goats, bemusedly watching the traffic. When I reached the top of the ridge, where the megalith stands, I stopped and got out of the car. It was cool up there, and very still. Not a breath of wind blew, as I climbed the little grass mound beside the standing stone.

Before me, over the tussocky moorland, the train stood at the frontier station, a thin plume of smoke rising vertically from its funnel, a clutter of cars and people all around. Once again I was reminded of Africa, where you sometimes see the big steam trains standing all alone, inexplicably waiting, in the immense and empty veldt. I looked behind me then, back over the peninsula: and like grey imperfections on the southern horizon, I saw the warships coming.

Trefan Morys, 1985